Exiled Alpha

Chloe Drill

Contents

1. Prologue — 1

2. 01 | Chosen Luna — 3

3. 02 | Threatened With A Cage — 9

4. 03 | Whispers Of Him — 15

5. 04 | The Bonding Ceremony — 22

6. 05 | She Hurt You — 31

7. 06 | Battle Of The Scents — 38

8. 07 | Hide And Seek — 45

9. 08 | Name Games — 52

10. 09 | Don't Get Attached — 60

11. 10 | Something Else — 68

12. 11 | You're Bipolar — 76

13. 12 | Bad Ideas — 83

14. 13 | Are You Jealous? — 90

15. 14 | Going Too Far — 97

16.	15 | A Different Breed	105
17.	16 | I'm Still Here	113
18.	17 | Demons	122
19.	18 | You Had A Choice	129
20.	19 | Sisterly Love	137
21.	20 | Humans Stink	145
22.	21 | Don't Be Petty	153
23.	22 | Only A Descendent	161
24.	23 | Things Changed	169
25.	24 | Considered Dead	176
26.	25 | Buried History	183
27.	26 | Understand Me	192
28.	27 | A Safe Place	198
29.	28 | Blood Of A God	206
30.	29 | Shattering Screams	214
31.	30 | Ruby Red Eyes	222
32.	31 | If We're Lucky	229
33.	32 | The Visarian Way	237
34.	33 | He Threatened You	244
35.	34 | Homesick	251
36.	Epilogue	258

Prologue

Three years ago, the world's strongest pack fell to a single blood crazed wolf. Nobody knew how one person could topple an entire territory. Or what he done to emerge victorious in the bloodshed that ensued. Nobody talked and nobody knew much of the one who became a tyrant seemingly in the blink of an eye.

One thing was for sure, and that's that in a mere few hours, the leading pack of the world had fallen. The Roman Empire wasn't built in a day. But it certainly fell in one.

After this wolf out of the shadows gained the title of Alpha, he held it quietly. Connections were cut off with his new pack. What happened within those borders were a mystery to the rest of the world. But rumors seem to have their way of spreading.

People talked of the new Alpha spilling blood at every turn. How he would slaughter dozens without even being provoked. That this one wolf was so absurdly powerful that he ruled by himself: no Luna, no Beta, no adversaries. Yet nobody knew what drove him.

Three long years this went on. Eventually any more news of the pack fell silent. Until one day, it becomes loud. That day, something happens that shakes every werewolf to their core.

The tyrant Alpha is exiled.

Driven away from his own claimed territory.

The pack struggled to rebuild after that, left Alpha-less and weak. But they were no longer anyone's concern. The world had their eyes on the one whom they threw out instead.

Word spread rapidly that the Exiled Alpha is with a vengeance. That he roams the woods, trespassing from territory to territory just looking for another pack to conquer. To rule.

Every wolf across the globe quivers. On edge and paranoid. Doing whatever they can to prepare themselves, to ward off the monster lurking somewhere out in the woods.

And the Visari pack is no exception. Although their new Alpha has a different approach to the threat. And that is to take a Luna to fortify the pack's leadership. The more leaders, the more intimidation to outsiders. Right?

01 | Chosen Luna

S now crunches under my feet as I walk along the mountain path. The hoot of an owl mixes with the faint voices of people partying in the valley below. I envy them. They get to celebrate the exact thing that's caused me three mental breakdowns and a stomach twisted with dread.

I sigh, slowing my pace. I can't stop it at this point. But I'll sure as hell stall for as long as I can.

Maybe the alternative isn't so bad. Being invisible and ignored might be better than being tied to a narcissistic asshole.

I come to a high point in the trail and step off of it. A moth flutters up from a patch of tall, dead grass. It dances around in front of my face for a second before disappearing up into the black, starry sky until it's too small to see anymore. Likely off to hide somewhere else. I'm jealous of its freedom. It can hide from its problems. I can't.

Through a gap in the trees I look down to where the pack members are preparing in the clearing. Their bonfire is burning bright and tall, disrupting the otherwise black shadows and creating a spot of warmth among the cold landscape. Even with the distance, I can see the snow sparkling in the firelight.

A beautiful winter night has never looked so ugly.

• • •

4 Days Earlier...

"This one or this one?"

I wonder if squirrels live in neighborhoods. If a squirrel lives a couple trees away from another, does that make them neighbors? Or what if a squirrel builds a nest in a tree that already has one? Do they fight or do they coexist?

"Adrienne? Opinion?"

They probably get along. They probably go over to each other's nests and ask to borrow sugar. No, not sugar. Acorn dust... like squirrel cocaine.

A hard smack to my leg makes me jump.

"OW! What the hell?!" I rub my burning thigh and give Aimee a death glare. What did I do to displease Her Highness now?

"You aren't even paying attention! You're laying there staring at the ceiling like a washed up cucumber," she accuses. So maybe I'm not giving her my undivided attention. She has a fair argument there. But in my defense she can usually carry on a conversation just fine with herself as long as I give the occasional nod and grunt of acknowledgement.

I realize she's standing in front of me, holding a silver and black dress in each hand. After a quick game of eeny, meeny, miny, moe I point to the black one in order to avoid further abuse.

That simple action is all it takes to perk her back up.

"Great. I thought so, too," she says. She hauls the dresses back across the room, hanging the silver one in the closet and draping the black one across the back of an armchair.

"You know I really wish you would go to this party with me. Make some friends. It would do you good to talk to someone else besides me for once," she lectures as she plops down at her vanity. She opens a small glass bottle and starts smearing skin-colored paint on her face. It matches her cocoa tone perfectly.

"I'm starting to regret doing that much," I grumble in return. Aimee is the only person I truly consider a friend. I've known her for about as long as I can remember, though it wasn't until about a year and a half ago that we became close.

"Oh please. Your bitch ass loves me and you know it. And since you love me so much, you should come with me." Her words are mumbled as she puckers her lips to slather her dark purple lipstick on.

I don't waste time in shooting her down. "Not a chance."

"Oh, come on! It'll be fun. I hear Oarcan boys are a sight to see. Tall and sleek. With water dripping from their silky hair, down their chiseled abs and right to their-"

I gag. I actually gag. When that's not enough to stop her, I throw myself into an exaggerated coughing fit to get the point across. The last thing I need to hear about are Aimee's fantasies. Her many, many fantasies. And believe me when I say they're sickening. Her ones for the males of the Oarca pack-- another tribal pack, whose members have a special affiliation with water-- are exceptionally disturbing.

"You can act grossed out all you want now. One day is coming when the high and mighty Adrienne Gage is going to find someone attractive. And when you do I'll be there to rub it in your face." She pauses from meticulously tracing over her eyebrow with a pen. An ornery smile is stuck on her face as she looks in the mirror to see my reaction.

I roll my eyes. I'm skeptical. Extremely skeptical. Aimee embraces her sexuality fully, while I on the other hand, am not interested in the subject. Yet somehow we still get along, despite being the equivalent of polar opposites.

"Yeah, whatever." I stand up from her bed, grabbing my black jacket. "I'll see you later."

She looks up at me with one eyebrow matching her chocolate colored hair and the other barely visible under all the other products that are professionally caked on.

"Where are you going?"

"I have to help clean up for the party. Another celebration for that mightier-than-thou asshole I'm assuming. Who knows what for now," I say bitterly. My blood nearly boils with irritation just by thinking of that spoiled brat. In addition to that, I can feel my hair already falling out with the thought of putting up with Anthony the rest of the day.

Aimee laughs. She's always found my hatred for that asswipe to be entertaining. Needless to say, I don't find it so amusing. Just looking at him makes me homicidal.

"You can always come with me," she chimes with a cheery voice, wiggling her one visible eyebrow.

I snort and turn to leave. "Okay, laugh it up. You're next on the list."

• • •

The sun is warm against my back, making it seem more like mild fall than early winter.

"You missed a spot," Anthony nags for the millionth time from down below.

I can feel my patience deteriorating.

"Does it look like I'm done?" I glare down with the hatred of a thousand suns where he's busy steadying the ladder and critiquing my every movement. Even the top of his head— covered by moderately long, brown hair— annoys me.

I've never liked Anthony. He's the kind of person that could drive a Buddhist to take a swing at him. I'm not sure why this unlucky fate picked me as it's target, but I somehow always end up getting stuck with him, be it pack errands or border patrols.

"No, but you should get it before you forget. Right there, up in the corner." His innocent, completely clueless tone of voice only makes him all the more irritating.

I clench the sponge tighter, causing all the water to run out and down my arm. "Shouldn't you be hanging ribbons or something?"

"I'm just trying to help you, okay? This party is for you, you know." He points to another spot on the second story window that I've been cleaning for half an hour because it's impossible to satisfy this annoying freak.

"For me? What do you mean for me? It's for Nathan just like everything else." I say, scrubbing the window like I have a vengeance to settle with it.

Nathan is the Alpha's son. Along with his upcoming 18th birthday, the title will also be given to him. And just like all Alpha children, Nathan's a spoiled brat. Anything we ever do as a pack is always for him.

One time his father even made us throw a party for his first chest hair. What was even worse is that it was a dinner party. Of course I couldn't eat anything without throwing it right back up because one thought was always on my mind, and that was the fact that we were celebrating a chest hair.

"You haven't heard? Nathan picked you as his Luna."

Right then my foot slips off the ladder, sending me plummeting downward. My stomach is skinned on the steps before my hands gain purchase where my feet once were.

"WHAT?!" I choke on my own saliva while trying desperately to reattain my footing.

"I thought you would've known by now," He shrugs simply.

"No. There's nothing to know, because it's not happening." I state firmly and begin to climb down the ladder.

"Wait what are you doing? Adrienne we're not done! Adrienne!" His yelling falls on dismissive ears because there's no way in hell I'm walking back there, or letting this happen to myself.

There's a lump stuck in my throat and I'm so angry that my jaw quivers if I'm not grinding my teeth together. My stomach is in knots, but not the good, excited kind of knots. Instead, it's the kind of knots that urge breakfast to make a reappearance.

I storm my way towards the Alpha's house, on the hunt for a certain ego inflated, soon to be Alpha. The angry and quick pace I keep earns me some concerned stares from the pack members as I march through our little village.

I try to ignore them as I make a beeline for the house. Now that I think of it, everyone has been treating me differently. I've been getting dirty looks and side-eyed glares all week, and I'm just now noticing it.

They could only be thinking one of two things. Why her or thank the gods it's not me.

02 | Threatened With A Cage

My face burns with embarrassment and ignorance. Apparently, everyone has known about my fate except for me. But that ends now.

After having burst through the door of the Alpha's house without a single trace of hesitation, I head for the stairs where I know his office is. I'm marching my way down the hallway when angry voices stop me dead in my tracks.

"That maniac is on the loose! How am I suppose to takeover when he's out there just waiting for someone to pounce on?" I recognize the whiny yet still smug voice of the celebrated prick, Nathan Swelter.

Since I need to talk to him anyway, sticking around by the partially open door wouldn't be that wrong, would it? I've never exactly been against eavesdropping before, so what's the difference now?

That's my reasoning as I creep closer to the door and press my ear against the wall, letting the gift of heightened hearing do it's job.

"He's less likely to bother us if there are two leaders. You have a Luna picked out, correct?" I recognize the voice of Alpha Andre, speaking in a composed tone.

"I want Adrienne," he responds almost immediately, causing me to physically restrain the gag squirming to escape my throat. At the mention of my name, I feel the color drain from my face. "She's the one and I'm tired of waiting for both her and my title."

A deep hum reaches my ears, what the Alpha always does when he's considering something. "Then wait no longer. I'll have the wedding moved up to Thursday. Since there's no mate bond to bind you, vows will work just as well. Plus, you'll have more time to get acquainted with her. Maybe even-"

"There's not going to be a wedding," I announce, seething after barging through the door on impulse. There's no way I can stand out there and silently listen to my future being decided for me. Not anymore. I'm sick of being a ghost in my own life.

Two pairs of eyes turn on me. One is Nathan's-- a light blue that pairs nicely with neatly combed black hair. The other pair are a darker blue and belong to his father, whose once inky black hair is now peppered with grey. Evidence of the stress that comes attached to the title.

"Excuse me?" Alpha Andre stands up from his leather office chair. He has squared shoulders and a tall stature that would be hard to beat. One thing is for certain, and it's that he's used to looking down on people, not vice versa. He shoots me that disappointing gaze that he's mastered over the years, making even the most arrogant of wolves ashamed of themselves.

I swallow, fighting to keep my attitude under control. Too many times I've mouthed off to him and seen the consequences. But keeping this new leaf turned over is proving to be quite challenging.

"I'm not marrying him or anyone else," I seethe again, planting my feet firmly in place. He can't possibly think that he can force me into this. Can he? He's held control over me my entire life, but surely there's a line he won't cross. There has to be.

To my right, Nathan lets out a frustrated moan.

"Why can't you just cooperate for once?" He whines at me. "I thought we were past this. I can give you everything you want! Who turns down the title of Luna?" He looks to his father for help with pleading yet demanding eyes.

He's never grown up. He still reminds me of that same child who threatened to throw a tantrum if he didn't get his dessert. Or the one who threatened to have my fingers cut off if I tried to play with a toy he'd forgotten he even had.

"You can't give me shit or you wouldn't have treated me like it my whole life," I shoot back, feeling a growl starting to rumble deep in my chest. He's always thought of himself as royalty and everyone else peasants. But in my eyes, a king without a crown isn't a king at all.

Alpha Andre snarls at me for my backlash. "Watch your damn tongue." He then turns to his son, confidence thick in the air around him. "She'll do whatever I say." He sits back down in his chair, leaning back and watching me with a calculating look. One that reminds me of a beady eyed snake in the grass.

"Won't you Adrienne?" He asks in that sickly sweet, ominous voice. I hate that voice, that tone. I hate it with all of my being and I always have. It makes me sick. Sicker than imagining a future with Nathan.

I clench my jaw tightly, my hands curling into fists. "And if I don't?"

He tilts his head down and smiles darkly, clasping his hands loosely together. "Then you'll be locked up again. You wouldn't want that, would you? I'd think it gets awful lonely down there."

My blood turns to ice and suddenly I feel cold. Chilled to the bone. It's as if I can already feel the frigid stone against my skin and the silence ringing in my ears.

I hide my fear and scoff, skeptical and taken aback. There's no way I can go back there, not to that hellhole. Though if he's serious about this, then I'm more screwed than the missing ones in his head. Though that's an easy accomplishment.

"You wouldn't." I force my words to come out as a challenge, yet on the inside I feel like breaking down, dropping to my knees, and begging to keep my freedom.

He smiles again, his eyes sparkling with a twisted amusement. "Oh but I would."

He enjoys this. I know he does.

I find myself staring down at my shoes. Heat rushes to my cheeks at the fact that he can bend me so easily with one simple threat.

This can't be happening...

"The wedding is Thursday," the Alpha's words are like a cold bucket of reality, reassuring me that this isn't a nightmare. "That should be enough time. Now go on. I believe you have ceremony to prepare for."

Go figure. Forced into an engagement and I'm still the one who has to cater the party I don't want.

My feet move mechanically towards the door, more than ready to leave. But not without knocking a potted plant off a nearby table first. The sound of the clay shattering on the floor is amplified by the thick silence of the room.

"Bitch," I mumble under my breath.

"What was that?" Nathan snaps. It surprises me that he doesn't let his daddy handle this for him, too.

I start to prepare a sarcastically sweet response, but instead I decide to voice my true feelings. There's no longer a reason to keep my mouth shut.

I whirl around on my heel to face him. My eyes lock with his, shooting daggers dripping with venom.

"Bitch. That's what I said," I snap, loud and clear, "You're a fucking bitch and I hope and pray that one day comes when your rotting and bloated body is found floating in the river, eyeless because the fish have already picked them out."

It feels as though my skin is on fire and my lungs ache for air. I mean every single word of what I say and my tone is more than laced with hatred; it's seeping it. Pure and livid hatred.

I don't wait to see if he's going to patronize me further or if his father is going to throw me back underground for not holding my tongue. I slam the door behind me with enough force and intent that a loud crack through the wood streaks across it.

Instead of going back to prepare for the party like I'd been told, I head straight to one of the many smalls cabins in the village and into my bedroom, which is similar to a loft.

Fairy lights hang around the tops of the dark grey walls. The room is flooded with natural lighting from the giant window that my bed is sidled up against. I plop down on it, burying myself in the sheets.

Just forget it. Forget everything.

Forgetting is always easier. Except this time, I can't push the dreadful thoughts away.

The wedding is Thursday. That leaves me with four days. Four days left of freedom. Four days left to figure out how to save myself.

Suddenly, in a random thought, I remember what Nathan said before I barged in.

"That maniac is on the loose! How am I suppose to takeover when he's out there just waiting for someone to pounce on?"

What maniac was he talking about? And what does that have to do with him needing a Luna before he becomes the Alpha?

03 | Whispers Of Him

The sun is starting to sink down, casting a dim light over the bare trees and white sparkling mountains. The air is cold, invigorating.

I walk along a snow dusted path leading out of our little village and into the woods nearby. Large trees, somehow still full with leaves, form a circle around the clearing.

Aimee is standing against the shadowy tree line. A group of girls, none of which I've ever bothered to have a conversation with, are surrounding her. Their voices are low, kept in hushed tones that only signal one thing: gossip.

I perk my ears, listening in.

"I hear he's ruthless. A monster who's wolf is three times the size of any other Alpha," a petite, bleach blonde— Mya— whispers, her eyes wide for emphasis.

Her brunette friend shudders before giving her input. "They say he's an absolute beast. He goes out commits mass murder whenever he feels like it!" Suddenly she lowers her voice even more and it turns shaky, "God, what if he comes here? Who knows where the hell he is right now."

They all exchange wide eyed glances, looking to gauge each other's reactions.

Who the hell are they talking about? And why are they so jittery?

As I approach, a stick snaps under my heel. All of them jump, including Aimee who has seemed fearless for as long as I've known her. Mya even lets out a choked scream.

All of their eyes turn on me as if I were the devil come to claim their souls. Their faces ghostly pale and their mouths are agape.

"Goddamn it, you can't do that!" Mya shrieks at me, her face turning into an accusatory stare. Something about her tone cuts right through me.

I narrow my eyes and push my lips into a snarky pucker. "If you're so scared then why don't you go choke on something besides fear?"

She sucks in a sharp breath, taken aback. Maybe it was a bit too far, but I can't say that I'm sorry. Nathan has already frayed my nerves for the day. Mya's mouth gapes like a fish out of water as she tries to find her words.

"You know what, fuck you," she spits before storming off. The other four girls follow her off, scowling at me at they go.

I brush it off and turn my attention back to my best friend. Aimee remains standing with her back towards the trees.

"What was that all about?" I ask, walking up to her and pointing a thumb back at the group.

She isn't phased by the little scene she just saw between me and Mya. At one point she tried to teach me how to keep my inner thoughts inside. Needless to say, she never did succeed. Now she doesn't even pay attention to my lack of a filter as she raises an eyebrow, her forehead wrinkling.

"You haven't heard?"

I shake my head, furrowing my brow. I need to know what's going on. People gossip all the time, but never like this. Never with such fear.

"They call him the Exiled Alpha," she pauses in order to look up at the sky as it grows increasingly darker. "Shit, I have to go. I'm already running late."

Her sentences are rushed as she bends down to grab the strap of a purple backpack and heave it onto her back.

"Wait! What do you mean Exiled-"

Before I can finish she reaches out and grabs me firmly by the shoulders, looking me dead in the eye with such intensity that I feel paralyzed.

"Listen to me Adrienne," she squeezes my shoulders, speaking firmly, "I don't have time to explain right now, but just— don't go off into the woods by yourself. I know you like to, but don't. Stay near the pack. You understand?"

I catch a chill running up my spine; one that's not caused by the cold. I can only think one thing in that moment, and it's what the fuck is out there?

I don't understand. I have no idea what she's talking about, only that whatever it is is dangerous. But I nod anyway.

This seems to be good enough for her because the next thing I know, she's pulling me into a hug.

"Stay safe, bitch," she says beside my ear. So much for her seriousness.

She lets me go and steps away. When she does she's wearing one of her signature ornery grins. Usually that gesture would comfort me, seeing her back to normal instead of spewing warnings at me. But it doesn't. Because her smile is half forced.

"Sorry I can't stay for the party. Looks like you'll get Nathan all to yourself," she teases sarcastically.

A pang of anger shocks my stomach and I open my mouth with intent of spitting profanities at her. But I bite my tongue as realization hits me.

She doesn't know.

She doesn't know about the blackmailed engagement or wedding. If she did, she would have told me. I know she would've. And she would've kicked Nathan's ass, regardless of the consequences.

I force an empty smile back to her, not quite as convincing as her own.

Let her have her fun, I think, My problems aren't hers.

"Yeah whatever," I call back as she gets farther and farther away, "Just don't get aids."

She turns around just brief enough to stick her tongue out at me in a playful sneer.

I let out a heavy sigh when I turn around and start walking back. There are a couple people bustling about, a lot of them carrying various ribbons or decorations.

I walk past all of the working wolves, heading back to my room.

If Nathan or Andre either one expect me to prepare for the party of my own demise, then they're out of their minds. What could they possibly do to me? Sentence me to a lifetime of misery?

Oh wait...

• • •

It's been three days since Aimee left. Three days that I've been locked in my room, trying anything to keep my mind off reality.

The only time any part of me left the room is when I stuck my head out the window to smoke, not wanting the smell to stick to the walls. The little glass ashtray on my desk is full and two empty cigarette packs lay in the trash can.

At least four times a day, one of the lower ranking members, a maid or a servant, would bring me food. My only guess is that this is Nathan's way of trying to suck up. Feigning sweetness in hopes that I won't act out during the ceremony.

What he doesn't know though, is that his pathetic attempt to win me over is in vain. I won't bend for that asshole no matter how much food he sends to me.

I hadn't even realized I was letting myself drift to sleep until a knock on the door stirs me awake.

Each time food was delivered, someone called out to me after knocking. No voice follows this one.

Now what is it? Let me guess, I have to plan the bridal shower?

They knock again, this time louder.

"I'm coming," I growl, untangling myself from the sheets. I stumble my way over to the door and open it.

Nathan is standing there, hands in his pockets and a polite smile on his face. "Well hey there, sleepy head," he chirps. His tone is so nice that I can almost feel the bile rising in my throat. "The party's starting in half an hour. So look your best. It is in our honor after all."

I narrow my eyes and step back, looking him up and down. "Who the hell are you?"

He laughs, as if that were the funniest thing he'd ever heard. A cheerful sound, but also a fake one. "I just came to remind you," he says with in overly friendly tone before turning business-like, "Now do something with your hair, put on something expensive, and meet downstairs in ten minutes."

I don't move. Instead I stand like a statue, keeping my skeptical stare focused on him.

"Okay, look. As my chosen Luna, you have to have a look that makes everyone jealous of you on sight. Of course they'll already do that as long as you're on my arm, but still. I expect you to act like a perfect sweetheart, and if not... there will be consequences."

And just like that, the act is up. His conceited and bossy attitude is back in full swing, along with that pulsing vein in his neck. It always makes an appearance when he doesn't get his way.

I continue staring at him with dead eyes, knowing it would eventually make that nerve of his crack. If he intends to try and control my life— which he does— then he'll at least have to give me his reasoning.

"Why am I your chosen Luna?" I ask, suspicious. It doesn't make sense to me. We don't get along anymore, so why would he want to marry me? Against my will at that.

He smirks, meeting my eyes with a devious gleam of his own. "You're mouthy, Adrienne Gage. A sharp tongue and a clever head. That's what people can't see until it's already too late."

He moves closer, lifting my chin with his thumb. With less than an inch between our cheeks, his hot breath fans over my ear as he speaks in a low whisper. "And I can't forget those grey eyes... They're so cold. So unpredictable. So... unreadable."

He swipes his thumb across my jaw as he steps away, turning and leaving just like that. "Remember," he calls, his voice echoing in the dark hallway, "Ten minutes."

My fingers raise to touch where he did. I rub the skin until it starts to burn. I'm quite certain I've rubbed it raw with my palm, yet it still doesn't feel clean.

So that's his reason.

He plans to use me as his pawn.

But I'll be damned if I help him win whatever chess game he thinks he's playing.

With Alpha Andre's threat in mind, I close the door and get to work on myself reluctantly. If only I had a fashion savvy best friend like all the movies portray, then this would be a lot easier.

The cruel thing is is that I do; except she's miles away, partying her ass off in another pack.

At least one of us is having a good time.

-

Sorry for the late update! Hope you guys like it. I've decided to try to post every Friday and maybe Tuesdays.

Thanks for reading!!

04 | The Bonding Ceremony

I comb through my long hair, letting it hang down my back. Working against the clock, I throw on a pair of dark jeans, leather boots, a white t-shirt, and a black jacket. He said to wear something expensive, but this event can be called a high class cook out at best.

Technically, it's a bonding ceremony, which is the equivalent of a wedding to humans except without all of the elegance, fancy clothes, and decor.

Just like Nathan said, I find him waiting for me in the living room of the pack house. He stops his pacing in order to look me over from head to toe.

"How much did that cost?"

"Enough," I answer as I walk past him.

"Is it designer?" He asks, coming up beside me.

"It is for tonight."

He makes a disapproving grunt. "We'll go shopping later. You look good though."

I stop dead in my tracks, stiffening.

Did he... Did he just compliment me?

He offers me his arm, as if nothing out of ordinary had just happened. "Wouldn't wanna be late."

I wipe the petrification off my face and force myself to take the arm he's offering. It's an internal fight to keep myself from pulling away from him. Something about having any sort of contact with him seems wrong and stomach-churningly unappealing.

When we walk up to the open forested area that the party is set up in, everyone's eyes turn on us. The urge to shrink down and out of their sight is crippling, but there's nowhere to go. Plus I have too much pride to even attempt to hide against Nathan's side. Public shame can only go so far and that would be on an entirely new level.

There's no doubt in my mind that this is the latest gossip of the pack. The oh so beloved Nathan Swelter— soon to be Alpha of the Visari pack— is claiming a mate who isn't his.

He leads us past a towering bonfire whose flames reach high into the dark sky and to a long table set on a wooden platform which acts as a makeshift stage. There are four seats at the table, all at one side so that the occupants would all face the crowd.

Alpha Andre and his Luna, Nathan's mother, sit together at one end. I break away from Nathan and go past them, planting myself at the furthest end, as far away from them as I can be. To my misfortune, Nathan sits down next to me, far closer than I'd prefer.

No more than half a minute passes before he places his hand on my knee and starts tugging at my leg. I shoot him a burning glare so heated that he should burst into flames on the spot.

"Seriously?!" I snap, keeping it at a whisper.

He growls lowly, leaning closer. "You're mine now. Show it."

I clench my canines together so hard that my jaw aches. I roll my eyes and huff before throwing away my dignity and following his orders, lifting my legs so that they're in his lap.

It's a Visarian display of ownership. While sitting, the female would position herself so that the back of her thighs touch the top of the male's, though her butt stays in her own seat. In intimate cases, only between true mates, the male would wrap his arm around the female, her head resting on his shoulder.

However, that's not the case for us.

I put my thighs on top of his, but other than that, I keep as much distance as possible. It wouldn't be hard for someone to figure out that we're not mates. The stiff body language, the tense and mechanical movements, and not to mention my obvious disgruntlement; it's enough to make any spectator cringe with second hand embarrassment.

And of course, there's plenty of them to do so. Practically the entire pack is staring at us from below, unblinking. Despite the cold winter air, my face is on fire.

"Act natural," Nathan scolds in my ear.

"Maybe if I weren't being blackmailed I could," I hiss back.

Alpha Andre stands up, clearing his throat and sending us both a scolding look. He then slaps on a pleasant smile and faces forward to address the pack.

"Wolves of Visari, may I introduce to you to your soon to be Alpha and Luna," he announces, making a grand gesture towards us.

His speech goes on after that. Most of it, if not all of it, is him rambling on about Nathan's childhood and his meager yet exaggerated achievements.

Not a single thing is said about me. It's almost like he completely forgot that I could've been considered his daughter at one point. I'm not surprised though.

Nearly half an hour of empty words and transparent compliments later, he concludes his speech with something along the lines of "may he reign long and prosper with this pack."

Applause bursts from the crowd when Alpha Andre sits back down. Although I tuned out the majority of his speech, I highly doubt the applause is sincere.

When the clapping starts to fade, a single hand in the middle of the sea of people pops up.

"Nathan and Adrienne aren't mates. What happens when she finds her mate? Will Nathan then find a new Luna?"

I perk up upon hearing my name. But Nathan opens his mouth first.

"There will be no other Luna," he answers. My brow furrows when I realize his tone is almost... defensive? Who knew he was such a good actor.

He continues, and slowly the defensiveness dissipates into professionalism. "I chose Adrienne. The ceremony will bind us. And if her mate has a problem with it, he can either get over it or take it up with me."

I shiver. There's something about talking about my hypothetical mate that seems unnatural. Wrong even, and I don't like it.

There were no more questions after that. I was beyond thankful. The sooner this torture is over, the better.

Pack members begin passing out the food, giving me the dreadful cue to talk to the Alpha's asshole-ish offspring.

"When did you turn into plastic?" I ask him.

He looks at me, confused. "What?"

"You're fake, Nathan. Just like your little declaration of caring about me."

His gaze hardens and his jaw tightens, like I've hit a nerve. That's good though. Because I'd sever it if I could.

"I'd watch your fucking attitude if I were you," he warns dismissively.

I glance down at his palm resting right above my neck, then back up to him. "And I'd watch your hand if I were you," I growl, my teeth turning to canines.

Various dishes are sat down in front of me, all of them fresh and steaming. But none of them are bribing enough to make me stay.

"Where are you going?" Nathan asks as I abruptly stand up, having not even touched my a single morsel of food.

I mumble a bitter retort, one I'm sure he can hear, "For a walk, get off my back."

I don't look back, not even after hearing the rattling of silverware when a palm slams down on the table. Growling follows, low and provoked.

I guess now we both know what it's like to be inconvenienced by someone else.

"Let her go," Alpha Andre orders. I can just imagine him grabbing his son's wrist and pulling him back down before he can even get up. He's controlling like that. Except this time, I'm thankful for it.

• • •

Darkness hangs heavy in the sky, though the dim moonlit makes the snow on the ground sparkle. Pointy and crooked shadows are cast down from the limbs of the trees above.

My hands are burrowed into my coat pockets as I trudge along one of the many paths that are well burned into my memory.

I had stormed off and away from the party. I wanted— want— away from all of them. As I come to a high point in the mountain trail, I catch sight of the bonfire far below. Like a giant burning ember among the grey, bleak landscape.

Suddenly my stomach drops.

I temporarily forget all of my woes of dread as I remember what Aimee had said to me.

"Don't go off into the woods by yourself. Stay near the pack."

As if to go with my immense feeling of regret, my skin prickles with apprehension. Goosebumps pop up all over my arms, along with the hairs on the back of my neck rising.

Shit. Shit, shit, shit! Aimee would kill me if she knew I didn't listen. That is if this notorious lurking beast doesn't do it first.

I tense up, suddenly getting the feeling that I'm being watched. Though I know it's only a simple symptom of paranoia. Right?

I shake my head, laughing at myself. I'm acting as ridiculous as Mya and her group of floozies.

Either way, I turn and start back down the same path I came. The snow crunches loudly under my feet, almost like static in my ears that's loud enough to drown out everything else.

As I go back down the path, my mind goes back to reality. Dread settles in my stomach at the thought of going back to that asswipe whom his mother mistook for a person and named Nathan.

• • •

When I slip back into the vicinity of the party, I can't help but to notice the tense atmosphere of the people and their constant whispering. Or how their eyes are wide and flickering around as they talk to one another.

"It's true then? They really ran him out?" I overhear a hushed voice ask as I stop at the refreshments table.

Out of the corner of my eye, a tanned skinned girl, who I know as Trisha, bobs her head of curls with a nod. "They exiled him," she says quickly, "I didn't think they'd ever do it. Not after 3 years, especially."

What the hell is it with everyone whispering about this lately? What did Aimee say... the Exiled Alpha?

I busy myself to look casual, pouring a drink I don't even want.

"He's probably already looking for another pack to take over. Oh god, Trish, what if he's out there somewhere in the woods right now?! What if he smells the bonfire and-"

"Sophia, calm down," Trisha stops the other girl's increasingly hysterical rambling. "Just... Just don't think about it."

"Yeah. Yeah, you're right," She agrees, although her voice is quivering. "Hey. Hey, are you eavesdropping on us?!"

I look up to find a pale redhead staring accusingly at me, assumedly Sophia. I can't help but to notice the vibrant hot pink jacket she's wearing, along with a matching headband.

"I know it doesn't take that long to fill a cup," she continues, her eyes shooting daggers at me. Trisha, on the other hand, smiles apologetically, as if this sort of thing happens often.

I glance over at her before turning back to the table and picking up my drink. "You better keep your voice down. He might hear you," I mock as I start back towards my seat.

I have no idea who "he" is, but if it spites her, then so be it.

What happens next is nothing but a blur. While going back to my seat, I feel watched yet again. I look up to find Nathan's wide eyes staring at me. He stands up, his mouth agape and the color drained from his face. In the same instance that he points behind me, a bloodcurdling roar shakes the ground, followed by high-pitched screams.

I whirl around, coming face to face with Sophia, her arm raised in the air with something grasped in her hand. But that isn't what catches my attention.

Behind her, leaping out of the shadowy depths of the forest, is a monster beyond imaginable. An enormous, wolffish creature with glowing ruby red eyes. Even in midair it looks ten times the size of a normal wolf, and ten times as terrifying.

I don't even get the chance to panic or even so much as scream. The last thing I can process is a rock solid object crashing into my temple, erupting my skull in pain. Simultaneously, my vision plunges into blackness. Like somebody turned out the lights.

The last thing I saw was that beast coming straight towards me.

New chapter! Hope you guys like it! Tell me your predictions as to what this terrifying beast will do because I love reading the comments

Thank you so much for reading! It really does mean a ton to me :)

05 | She Hurt You

My eyelids flicker open, just barely enough to recognize the blurred blues, blacks, and whites of the night forest. I immediately notice the burning, sharp pain that's lighting my neck on fire with discomfort. Like there's canines sinking into my flesh and winning a tug-of-war match with gravity.

I'm... being carried? Like a fucking wolf pup?

Cold wind blows against my face, cutting right through my clothes and causing me to shiver.

Blindly I reach my hand out, trying to feel for anything at all. Warm fur tickles my palm, sending a jolt of electricity through my chest.

I remember what I saw. A giant wolf leaping out of the woods, roaring louder than any monster ever could.

A sort of drugged, calm fear comes over me. I don't want to face this thing, whatever the hell it is.

So I close my eyes and let the safety of the darkness seep back in.

•••

I wake up to a pounding ache in the left side of my skull, right above my temple. My eyes open, which makes the pounding worse. Out of instinct, my hand reaches up to the source of the pain. Instead of oozing blood like I'd expected, I'm surprised to feel the soft gauze of a bandage wrapped securely around my head.

I roll my head to the side to take in my surroundings. Through the trees, in the distance, a bright orange flicker stands out against the night.

The bonfire. I can barely see it through the trees. How did I get out here so far?

Sitting up, I close eyes close tightly as I wait for the spinning to stop and the nausea to pass. When I finally open them again, my heart stalls.

Staring straight at me is a complete stranger. Though strange is far from the word I'd use to describe him.

As soon as my eyes lock with his, all of my senses immediately pulse in unison, shaking me to my core. All my attention is on him and only him. His smell, his looks, and even the pleasant rhythm of his heart in my hyperactive hearing. Or maybe that's just mine beating violently out of my chest.

He's sitting cross legged on the forest floor, leaning forward as if to get a closer look at me. His eyes are a pure obsidian color, and they hold an uncanny resemblance to the glowing red ones I vaguely remember. His messy hair is a brownish copper, which matches the thin layer of clean cut stubble on his perfect jawline.

Even with the small bit of distance between us, it's clear that his build is larger than an average person's. Not to mention three times as muscular.

I can't even try to think straight. He's attractive in a way no one person should be allowed to be.

His fingers flex in and out, the tendons in his wrists popping up along with some veins in his forearms. Judging from the raw power stored in that action alone, it would be ridiculously easy for him to take a life away.

Those hands look like they could bring death in a dozen different brutal ways— and I feel like they have. Yet for some reason, I yearn to reach out and touch them.

The pulsing sensation gets stronger, making my focus on him so heightened that everything else is dull.

My lips part slightly, but no words come out. Instead it gets stuck in the front of my mind, lingering at the tip of my tongue.

Mate.

I flinch at the word.

He makes a move to get up and I scramble backwards on my butt, fighting my every instinct to go forward.

My back meets the smooth trunk of a snow covered, fallen beech tree. It blocks me from going any further and I exhale heavily. Of course that's my luck.

He's coming slowly toward me, making my breath hitch. From a standing position his size looks impossibly larger, and impossibly like a force not to be reckoned with.

His nostrils flare as he sniffs the air. A low growl rumbles in his chest, getting louder as it travels up to his throat. "You smell like him," he says in disgust, pushing it out through gritted teeth.

Him? Does he mean Nathan?

But if that bothers him, then that makes two of us.

"And you smell like a wet dog," I retort without missing a beat. That was a lie. That was the biggest lie I've told in my entire life.

He smells good. Really good. Like an addictive, masculine cologne mixed with the natural scent of a pine forest. And the fact that that scent makes my stomach twist with nerves scares me.

His gaze burns into me, telling me I made a mistake. The lighting in his dark eyes seems to dance, like a black and grey fire burning in his irises. It's as though it signifies a battle of some kind... like he's fighting with his own inner wolf.

"What are you to him," he finally asks, the growl still in his voice.

"Why does it matter," I fire back. My wolf may already trust him, begging for his arms to encompass me, but I can't say the same.

He takes another step forward, hands clenching into fists. "Answer. The. Question."

I stay silent for what feels like centuries. Some part of me doesn't want to tell him the truth. Not only because it would be voicing my misfortune and misery, but also because I somehow feel like I've betrayed him.

"Where is everyone?" I ask instead, trying to change the subject.

His shoulders visibly tense, as if I've made him uncomfortable. For the first time, he breaks eye contact.

The way I see it, he doesn't have the right to be uncomfortable in this situation. I do.

He doesn't answer the question, which only makes my mind race faster. I happen to glance past him and a lump forms in my throat at what I see. The snow is disturbed and sprawled everywhere. Bright patches of red stain what was once sparkling white.

Among that, my eyes land on a piece of hot pink fabric laying in the middle of it. A headband.

I dare to venture further, looking even farther past.

A body is laid, sprawled and broken in the snow. I recognize the disheveled fiery red hair.

My blood runs cold.

"Did you...?" I don't need nor want to finish the sentence.

He follows my line of vision before answering with a simple, emotionless reply.

"Yes."

I swallow hard, feeling my hands start to shake. Goddamn it, why am I so nervous? If he wanted me dead he would've killed me while I was unconscious.

"W-Why...?"

"She hurt you."

As if on cue, my hand comes up to touch the bandage around my head. He cares if I'm hurt or not?

No response comes to mind for that. That girl didn't mean anything to me. She made snide comments about everything and walked over everyone. She was rude and a pain in the neck, but still... it doesn't seem believable.

But if Sophia is dead... who else went with her?

I hadn't even realized I was lost in thought, staring at the ground until the snap of a twig pulls me back to reality. My neck doesn't even have time to turn before I'm being scooped off the ground, pressed against a warm, solid body.

An electric sensation ignites wherever we touch, erupting my skin in a tingling, pleasant fire. It's like a chain reaction, making my heart start to pound again in my chest, along with my muscles relaxing instantly.

The logical part of my brain tells me I should be concerned about where he's taking me. But I can't focus on anything except his body against mine. My neck tilts to rest on his shoulder, the sensation lulling me into a state of tranquility.

Whether it's the possible concussion giving me hallucinations or not, I think I hear a faint, animalistic purr in response.

I close my eyelids, focusing on the smooth gait of his walk while being carried by arms that make me the equivalent of weightless.

It seems like minutes pass by before I open my eyes again. When I do, we're in the small village of my pack. I happen to look up, and in the second story window of one of the houses, half a dozen pairs of eyes are staring down at us.

Among them are Mya's. Her face is twisted with contempt, glaring hatred at me even through the glass. I can't be bothered to react this time.

I look around and notice that not a single person is outside. They're all in the windows, peaking out and watching us like hawks. It's almost as if they're scared of something.

What did they witness that I didn't? Besides Sophia's death...

I'm carried straight through the middle of the village, right to the grand cabin at the end; the one notoriously known as the Alpha's house. The stranger carrying me— my mate?— is unfazed. He continues on as if it's his territory. As if he has every right to be here.

He steps over the threshold of the front door, angling me carefully so that my feet don't hit the frame when we pass.

The entire pack just watched helplessly as a trespasser waltzed through our village, and stepped into the Alpha's house without a trace of hesitation.

What did he do to them?

The door clicks shut, plunging the room into darkness at the mercy of night.

But more importantly, my stomach knots as the stairs creak under the weight, what will he do to me?

-

Sorry there wasn't much dialogue this chapter! Trust me, you'll get to know "him" more later ;)

If anyone knows any good faceclaims do send them my way :)

What do you think he plans to do with Adrienne?

Thank you for reading!

06 | Battle Of The Scents

Dedicated to all the people who have been asking for updates <3

My heartbeat pounds in my ears as the bedroom door clicks shut behind us. This stranger has an iron grip on me, not to mention an aggressiveness that could terrify anyone.

I want so badly to feel safe in my mate's arms— to let myself relax against his warm chest. But I can't. Anxiety only grips me tighter as he carries me towards the bed. The sheets rustle quietly as he sits me down on the edge and begins pulling off my jacket. My heartbeat pulses in my throat as the panic begins setting in.

Once the jacket is off he tosses it onto the floor, almost in a disgusted manner. He pauses for a minute after that, raising his nose as if to sniff the air. I take this opportunity to squirm further onto the bed, and further away from him. I hug myself tightly and pull my knees halfway to my chest. Suddenly the white T-shirt that I'm left with feels much too thin for comfort.

I swallow nervously, watching as he walks over to an attached room and turns the light on, revealing a bathroom. My skin prickles as I watch, the saliva cold in my mouth.

What's he going to do?

In one swift motion he raises his arms over his head, peeling off his shirt. My eyes feel ready to bug out of my head.

I did not sign up for this.

The light behind him illuminates his figure, creating a sublime, muscular silhouette made of rigid lines and defined curves. I can only faintly see the center of his outline, but it's enough to tell that his abdomen is no less apparent.

Striding towards me, his steps are slow and confident. He stops in front of the bed, looking down on me with intent, dark eyes. I lean back as he reaches forward, but I don't lean far enough. His fingers touch under my chin, igniting the area with a tingling feel as he gingerly pushes my jaw closed.

Heat rushes to my cheeks when I realize my mouth had been open. Was it that obvious?

My eyes flick to his uncertainly. What happens now? Because there's no way in hell that I'm letting these clothes leave my body.

"Wash his scent off," he orders, his voice like steel. There's no denying that it's a command, not a polite suggestion.

He then drops his T-shirt carelessly into my lap. His voice is cold as he instructs me. Begrudging even.

"Then put this on."

With that, he lets his gaze linger for a few seconds. Then, he turns and strides out of the room, closing the door behind him with a loud click to disrupt the nerve wracking silence.

I scrunch my face up in both discontent and confusion.

He wants Nathan's smell off of me. That's the only conclusion I can come to, and a likely one considering his earlier disgruntlement with the scent. Being treated as a doll to be dressed up is irritating. But in this case, I don't want Nathan's scent on me either.

Cautiously, I slide off the bed, watching the door like a hawk. I half expect him to burst through it at any minute, spewing more demands.

With shirt clenched tightly in my hand, I pad into the bathroom, shutting the door behind me and making a point to lock it.

Mate or not, my privacy is my own.

The searing water is uncomfortable, drumming against my back, between my shoulder blades. My skin is burning to the point that I think it may peel off.

I've always preferred the cold. And I'd never choose a hot shower over a moderately room temperature or even a slightly cold one. But I need to feel the pain. I need to have the distraction it provides. Almost like it's a pause button.

I fight to keep my mind off the situation at hand, along with the questions that go with it. Did this stranger— my mate whose name is a mystery— take over the pack? How many of my pack members did he kill? Am I still expected to marry Nathan?

I shake my head, pushing away the curiosity. Whatever happens, happens. It's not like I was allowed to control my life before. What's the difference now?

My focus turns back to my reddening body as I turn the water off and step out of the shower. I'm shaky as I put my clothes back on, my muscles lulled into a trance from the heat. Even more warmth pools in my stomach when I take a deep breath of the addictive scent clinging to this ominous stranger's shirt.

I'm not a petite person per se, but it's still oversized to the point where I might be able to get away with not wearing anything else. Nonetheless I slip my jeans back on anyway. There's a certain line drawn in my dignity that I'm not quite ready to cross yet. And walking around pantless with a shirt tail barely covering my ass would require crossing that line.

When I reenter the bedroom, my lovely and very congenially mate is nowhere to be found.

Is this my window for escape?

As soon as the thought crosses my mind, I ridicule myself for such a ridiculous idea. Running away from everything I know just to be killed on sight as a rogue? I'd rather not. Yet, at least.

I wander out of the bedroom— which has to be the guest one considering its lack of a scent— and down the stairs, right out the front door I was carried through. The stranger doesn't stop me, nor is there even any sign he was here.

Outside, the entire village still looks deserted and desolate. Everything is dark, with only the moon acting as a dim lamp of silver light. The snow crunches beneath my feet as I wander through the empty streets— which are really just worn out paths weaving between the cabins.

My nostrils flare when a certain hair raising smell reaches my nose. Immediately goosebumps rise over my arms as I slow to a stop in the middle of the village, smelling the air more intently now.

Blood.

No... It's more than just blood. It's carnage.

If that smell, combined with the dark, soulless streets, isn't enough to send someone over the edge, then having your every move watched is.

Just as before, when I look up, I find the curious, frightened eyes peering at me through the windows.

A growl escapes my throat.

I'm some kind of spectacle for them, and that fact piques me.

I stare right back, but whoever it is doesn't budge.

If they won't come out, then I guess that means I'll go in.

The heavy door of the pack house shutting behind me is louder than it should be. Usually I would avoid drawing too much attention to myself, but between Nathan's ceremonies and whatever the hell this can be called, I haven't been left much of a choice.

When I turn the corner going into the grand living room, I'm met with about a dozen pairs of those staring eyes, glaring at me through the dark hue and blue shadows of the room.

"You're wearing his shirt?" Mya's irritating, high pitched voice exclaims as she throws her arms out dramatically. She's standing in front of one of the large windows beside the couch. There's no doubt that she was peeking out of it just a moment before.

I'm not sure what she's trying to imply by her comment, but it runs right through me nonetheless.

"You're clothed at all?" I regurgitate her exaggerated shock right back to her. More often than not, she's usually showing more skin than she's covering. And it's far from being subtle, which is why I'm surprised to find her covered from head to toe in winter apparel.

I can sense the room grow impossibly tenser. Everyone silently watching shifts uncomfortably in their seats and standing positions, but some of them I can feel staring holes right through me.

Mya crosses her arms and sneers. "You're calling me a slut but you're the one who just went to bed with a FUCKING TYRANT!"

I freeze.

Tyrant?

Then it clicks.

This is the tyrant everyone has been whispering about. The monster that Aimee warned me to stay away from.

So much for that.

"Enough, Mya," Alpha Andre growls, entering through the kitchen. His presence immediately weighs down the air, making it heavy with tension. "Adrienne," he motions past himself, gesturing for me to enter the room he just came from.

Alpha Andre may be the last bastard I want to talk to, next to his son, but I gratefully take the opportunity to get away from Mya. As I stride across the room to Andre, I stick my tongue out at her in a taunting sneer. She always hated being scolded by Andre instead of being his lap dog, and I've always loved her indignation over it.

Once in the kitchen, I clench my jaw when I see Nathan sitting at the table. There's no denying that I have strong feelings for him. Just not the feelings he wants me to. But repulse is a very strong feeling nonetheless.

Although repulse isn't what I get we approach the table. It's more like happiness. Because there's just something about of him, with his head down, held between his hands, with stress creasing his features, that's satisfying to me.

"Explain to us," Andre says, leaning past me to lay his palm flat on the tabletop, "What that monstrous bastard wants with you."

-

Predictions to what Andre and Nathan plan to do? Because certain someones got inflated egos and got their pack taken away :)

Also, a question: Do you guys think I should start giving the chapters names instead of just numbers?

Thanks for reading!

07 | Hide And Seek

Recap: "Explain to us," Andre says, leaning past me to lay his palm flat on the tabletop, "What that monstrous bastard wants with you."

...

"Explain to you?" I repeat, raising an eyebrow. "You're the ones who watched it happen!"

"And you're the one who he took into my goddamn house," Alpha Andre retorts coolly.

"So I'll say it again," he stands up straight as if to add an intimidation factor, "What does he want with you?"

I realize that I don't want to tell them. This thing between me and 'that monstrous bastard,' assuming it is what I think it is, is too personal to be ruined by Andre's opinion and Nathan's hatred.

So I play dumb instead.

"I don't know what he wants," I answer, adding an irritated tone to make it sound believable.

Andre hums as his eyes rake over me, from head to foot and back. Deciding whether to believe me or not. Whether to kill his prey or let it walk another day.

"That's his shirt," he observes, stroking his black and grey beard.

I notice his nostrils flare subtly, smelling.

"Did he make you wear it?"

I nod.

Half a minute passes by. Half a minute of Andre deep in silent thought and half a minute of Nathan and I in silent confusion.

Then, he speaks.

"You're the meat," he says.

"Come again?"

"He was watching the ceremony from the dark," he concludes, "He knows you're Nathan's chosen Luna. Taking his pack is one thing, but taking his Luna is a statement of further dominance. He's baiting Nathan to challenge him and you're the bait. The meat."

I blink, dumbfounded. His theory sounds... surprisingly reasonable? Probable even.

My stomach drops as I consider the possibility that he's right.

The feeling of stupidity heats my cheeks. Maybe I didn't know as much about this stranger as I thought. Maybe his ferocious desire to replace Nathan's scent with his own had a different motive than I thought. Maybe what I thought I felt for him was nothing at all.

Out of the corner of my eye, Nathan stiffens in his seat. His jaw is clenched without a doubt, and I'd bet money that the vein in his neck is just waiting to make an appearance.

"So he's toying with me?" Nathan growls, balling his fists on the table top.

Alpha Andre pulls out the chair opposite of his son and slumps down in it, stretching his long legs out. He crosses his arms over his chest and heaves a sigh. Three prominent stress lines crease the old Alpha's forehead.

"Riot Sydney doesn't toy with people. He destroys them."

A forceful shiver jerks my entire body and my breath audibly hitches in my throat. My chest is like a drum locked in a room with metal walls, every beat being echoed right back to it. The affect that this name has is terrifying.

Riot Sydney, I repeat in my head. The Exiled Alpha. That's his name.

My eyes blur out of focus as I remember his face. His perfect jawline covered with just the right amount of stubble. Stubble that I haven't gotten to feel against my skin or in my palm. His sharply cut nose and strong cheekbones. Somehow, there's something about everything about him— right down to that minuscule scar that cuts off the tip of his right eyebrow— that Riot Sydney fits perfectly.

An aggravated growl demands my attention. When I look up, Nathan's fierce glare is settled on me.

"You're thinking of him now? Because you think he's gonna win this game?" Although they're formed in questions, his touchy words are identical to an accusation.

I raise an eyebrow, taken aback by the confidence in himself. But of course he would have confidence. Assholes always do. And with his pompous need to have confidence comes my profuse need to crush it.

A devilish grin starts to pull at the corners of my lips.

I blow air out of my nose in a laugh, "How could he not? He's already taken your pack. Now what's dominating it to him? Nothing."

There's the angry vein that I've been waiting on.

I anticipated Nathan's reaction; irritation so beside himself that he bites his tongue and clenches his fists like a red-faced child trying not to have a tantrum. But Andre's, I didn't anticipate. Andre's, I didn't even think possible. Not for this.

A quiet growl rumbles in his throat as he slowly comes to sit up straighter in his chair.

"Nathan," he growls, not looking nearly as relaxed as he had five seconds ago, "Take her back to the cell."

The color drains from my face. My stomach twists so violently that I want to puke. My hanging jaw is trembling. Spasming. Visibly shaking.

"She won't be of use to him down there."

I take a step back.

"Don't fucking touch me." My voice is weak. So weak and unsteady.

Nathan reaches out to grab my arm. "Adrienne-"

"NO!"

I jerk back, backing toward the door. I register that the side of my face is twitching, involuntarily.

"Adrienne-"

"Shut up."

"Don't make this difficult."

I reach behind me and fling the door open, rushing out so fast that I nearly trip over my own feet. When I turn back, he's in the doorway, making a hasty grab for my arm. The door is slammed shut, and in the same instance a scream tears from the other side of it.

I see the shiny nails of four fingers sticking out before I turn and bolt thoughtlessly into the brush of the forest.

I hope they rot and fall off. Asshole.

• • •

The snow from the previous day is mostly gone, only a light dusting left on the frozen ground. The trees, leafless and bare, still provide hiding places, not that I'm using them.

My claws click against the hard dirt and frozen carpet of dead leaves on the forest floor. My heartbeat pounds to a frantic rhythm in my chest and hot breath heaves from my mouth, warming the clothes between my jaws.

I can hear him nearly a mile back. He's also breathing heavily, claws scratching the dirt every now and then with a faltered, lazy step. And sometimes, when the wind blows from behind me, I think, just maybe, that it carries the smell of his bloodied, broken fingers with it.

I remember this game from when we were kids. I remember playing hide and seek with the Alpha's son before he turned into a bastard. I was always better at it, because I knew the land better; every tree and every bush, memorized through every season. While he hardly left the village, I strived to get away from it.

But he never gave up then. And he won't give up now. Especially not now. Not when his daddy has given him an order.

My run slows to a jog, then to a walk, until eventually, I come to a stop and drop the clothes behind a mound of piled up brush. I sit for a handful of seconds behind the barrier of fallen limbs and sticks, catching my breath.

Taking in the deep and light browns of both the ground and the trees and brush surrounding me, I curse the sky for not having snowed the night before. Against this background, my cream colored fur is nothing but a white flag waving surrender.

I grit my teeth and bare the pain of my body shifting, exchanging fur for skin.

I all but get the dark jeans buttoned and the shirt pulled down before the hairs on the back of my neck rise.

He's near.

I suck in a sharp breath to shallow my breathing. But it's pointless.

An arm shoots from around the brush pile, it's hand grabbing the collar of my shirt. A gasp rips from my throat when I'm jerked sideways, pulled face to face with that piece of egotistical shit.

My hand wraps around his wrist, trying to crush it.

"Stop.. RUNNING!" He manages through heavy breaths. On instinct, I swing my free arm around, dragging my clawed fingers across his face with burning hatred.

If only it were his throat.

As soon as he expresses his pain— vocally, through a string of choice words— I break away and flee off into the woods once again.

If we keep on like this, maybe he'll bleed out first.

The frozen mud seems to bite at my feet, my boots having been abandoned at the beginning of the chase. It stings, no doubt the skin gradually being scraped off the bottoms.

I make a sharp turn and run a few more yards before picking a tree and feverishly climbing. Hiding is a long shot. I know that. But my folder of options is progressively getting thinner.

It's only when I drag myself up one last limb and lean my back against the trunk that I realize just how much fire is burning in my lungs and how shaky my hands are. I suck in air, breath after breath, hoping to cool the heat in my chest.

When I look down, a bright red in the corner of my eye catches my attention. On my collarbone, staining the brilliant white of Riot Sydney's t-shirt, is two drops of blood: one thumb sized and the other slightly smaller.

-

I feel like this chapter might be a bit boring but it was fun to write XD.

Do you think Andre's right about the tyrant using Adrienne as a statement against Nathan?

Thanks for reading!

08 | Name Games

My head jerks back up, something feathery and wet hitting my cheek. I brush away the fat snowflake and blink the sleep from my eyes.

It's had to of been at least an hour by now. Nathan's a persistent bastard but he won't hold out for this long, surely.

A sharp pain is shooting through my tailbone from sitting on the hard tree branch for so long, and the rest of my body is excruciatingly stiff. I grimace as I throw a leg over and sit up further to begin the climb down. It doesn't matter how ceased up or sore I am, anything out here is better than that cell.

My claws scrape into the bark as I slide down the trunk of the tree, groaning deeply as soon as my feet hit the ground and gravity becomes more of a reality. Giant flakes of snow float down around me, landing in my hair and sticking to my clothes as I stretch. The atmosphere has darkened, the sky turning a dreary grey.

Maybe he went back to his daddy with his tail tucked.

No more than a whole five seconds later and the loud snap of a stick snapping comes from the direction I had.

Of course. Daddy would be mad if he went back. And we can't have that, can we?

He won't leave me alone. Nathan may be a pompous ass, but he's a persistent one.

It becomes clear to me what my options are. I either stay here and get thrown back in that hellhole, or I leave. The only way I escape is if I start walking now and never turn back.

But there's nowhere to go. I'm oblivious to the world outside of Visari. I know that there's other tribal packs: Oarca, Bastieel, and Talonia. But I don't know their customs. I don't know their people or their land or their way of life. Everything is foreign beyond here.

Another sound, like a body pushing through vegetation, is closer now. Panic starts to set in, the tingling in my limbs urging them to take action.

He's getting closer. Quickly, undeniably, and terrifyingly closer.

I run. I run for all my miserable, wasted life is worth without any fucking idea where I'm going to. I just run.

Twigs snap at my ankles and my bare feet are yet again cold and pained on the frozen ground. But I'm not stopping. I don't care if I leave a trail of blood in my path.

It irks me that I can't shift, since four legs are infinitely faster than two. But shifting now would be like sounding the alarm for him to come find me. For whatever reason, a werewolf can sense whenever another one shifts nearby. It's a strange feeling, like a presence over your shoulder except the presence comes from the shifting wolf's location.

The next thing I know my shoulder is being plowed into the hard ground as a giant furry mass hits me from behind. I can feel the skin being scraped off my arm and elbow and the bloody wounds being filled with dirt and snow.

My jaw is slammed shut in the process. My teeth clamp down involuntarily on my tongue, sending tears to my eyes.

I don't even register the pain. Instead my attention goes to what's standing over me and pinning my back against the ground. And it's not Nathan's light grey wolf, either.

It's that giant, nightmarish monster I saw right before my pack was taken over. The one that drug me into the woods a paradox of gentle canines at the back of my neck. I never got a good look then, only a few glimpses through bleary, barely conscious eyes.

Now I have a good look, gaping up at it as it looks back with searing eyes.

I'm unable to move, staring petrified. I jerk when he moves his muzzle closer to my cheek. He smells it first, and then nudges the loose tendrils of hair aside with his cold nose.

A drop of blood slides down my face, leaving a warm, sticky trail all the way to my jaw. I realize there's a numb burning there, like a claw scratched into my cheek. I must have done it during the fall and not even noticed.

He starts to lick the wound, his soft canine tongue acting as a painkiller. The blood is wiped away and the burn starts to die out.

Once satisfied, he starts sniffing elsewhere, as of searching for my wounds. He makes a low growling sound when his nose stops just above my collarbone.

Right overtop of the two red stains; the stains made my Nathan's broken fingers.

Just as suddenly as he'd flatten me to the ground, he hurriedly steps off. For a split second, I think there's a flash of red in his eyes. But when I look again, it's gone.

As he turns away from me, I take the opportunity to stand up.

His wolf is a sight to cower at. Supernatural wolves by default are abnormally large, but there's something more looming about this one that I just can't explain. Even in a standing position he still casts a shadow over me.

When he turns back to me there's a subtle flash of light within his irises, followed by a quiet rumbling in his chest. Then he jerks his head in the direction of the village, staring me down with a threatening gaze. It's like he's accusing me of something.

He's angry with me. But why?

Then I realize. This is technically his pack now. And now he's caught me running away from it.

I wring my hands together nervously in front of my stomach. My heart is beating so loud that there's no way he can't hear it. But it's not from the adrenaline of the chase this time; it's from fear.

What will he do to me?

All the warnings I've heard whispered, all the craze, all the terror everyone has had for this wolf all pops into my head. What will he do? Judging by the stories, the possibilities are endless.

I take timid step backward.

A horrifyingly enraged snarl rips from his lips as soon as I do.

This radiance of power and aggression that he gives off, it's so strong that I can hardly control myself.

For the first time in my life, my instincts are telling me to cower. I just want to lay down and cover my head with my hands and hope for the best.

Yet I don't. I stay standing, staring at the ground in front of me and fighting the urge to close my eyes. When he starts to move towards me, with his enormous paws crunching the leaves beneath them, I tense up even further.

He circles me, walking around until I can feel his presence behind me. Then his nose prods me between my shoulders blades, forcefully shoving me forward.

He's taking me back to the village. And back to that cretinous asshole. Fantastic.

• • •

The entire way back he follows close behind— close enough for his hot breath to fan the back of my neck.

By the time we reach the the Alpha's cabin, which is assumedly his now, I feel like a prisoner. He escorts me right through the door, not offering the chance to falter a single step. My cheek is bleeding again and a dampness is on my hairline that I can't decide between being moisture from his breath, nervous sweat, or werewolf slobber. I settle for not knowing.

I'm guided through the large living room with, up the stairs, and down the hallway. He prods me in the shoulder with his nose for the hundredth time, silently ordering me to stop in front of the door to the guest room from before.

Taking the hint, I open the door and enter.

He gestures into the room with his head. Hesitantly, I walk further in, looking around. The door suddenly clicks closed, leaving me alone.

Now what? Does he expect me to do something here? Is he waiting for me to make a run for it again?

I sit down on the bed, sinking down in the plush comforter. I look at my lap, spacing out while mindlessly picking at the hem of my—his— shirt.

I'm still zoning out when the doorknob turns suddenly, making me jump in my own skin.

He's is standing in the threshold of the door. My eyes go directly to what's in his hands.

"What are you doing?" I blurt out with a bit of a squeak. I swallow nervously, watching his every movement like a hawk.

He approaches me, a long, thick rope hanging in his grip.

"Hold out your hands," he orders, standing in front of me now.

"Are you serious? You're gonna tie me up now?" I ask with a skeptical laugh. This might not be the time to be laughing, but are you kidding me?

He growls loudly and suddenly, making me yank my arms up in a heartbeat and hold them out at his mercy.

He starts by tying my wrists together, then my hands while my fists are balled, making it impossible to spread my fingers, and henceforth impossible to use my claws. He ties the opposite end of the rope to the bedpost, giving me leeway to move around a bit but never leave. Just like a dog on a leash.

He avoids eye contact the whole time he works, making me wonder if it's possible that he feels somewhat guilty for this.

The lighting of his obsidian irises is doing the flickering thing again, like his wolf is trying to come out but he's fighting to restrain it.

Typically, a werewolf's eyes only turn black when its primal instincts are triggered. His have stayed dark, which means he's been on the edge of losing control to his wolf this entire time.

He starts towards the door and I suddenly feel the need to stop him. Like some part of me wants him to stay, if only for a few seconds longer.

"Are you at least gonna tell me your name?" I ask indifferently.

I know his name. I've heard it off of Alpha Andre's tongue. But something, some part of me, needs to hear it off his.

He pauses with his hand over the light switch, not bothering to turn around. Even beneath the fabric of his shirt I can see the taut muscles of his back tightening.

"Riot Sydney."

A few seconds pass as the name sinks in. Goosebumps rise on my skin and entire body prickles with alertness. I visualize the spelling of it in my head and repeat it various times.

He looks over his shoulder, not at me, but exposing the side of his face in my direction. "What's yours?"

I'm quiet for a while before answering, "Why should I tell you?"

I say it mostly to annoy him, but partially because I truly don't see a reason to tell him. He doesn't deserve that yet.

"Because I told you mine," he growls, something he seems to do a lot. His fingers grip the frame of the doorway harder, causing the wood to crack loudly.

"So? I didn't offer you a trade," I huff as I lay over on my side and squirm to get comfortable. Which is a challenging task when unable to spread my arms at all.

Once settled, I rest my head on the pillow and close my eyes. "Goodnight," I say curtly.

It doesn't take long for the light to flip off and for the room to be bathed in darkness. Directly following that, the door slams aggressively closed.

Despite it, I can't find it in me to be scared anymore.

I lay there, fully ready to go to sleep, but something eats at my conscience.

In the back of my mind, I know that it's because he's angry with me. But I push that thought away.

I got the last word in and that's all that matters.

-

Thoughts on Riot's intentions/emotions?

I don't really know what other questions to ask...

Thanks for reading!

Oh yeah, I made a signature banner thing. Not sure how I feel about it.

09 | Don't Get Attached

Warning: half-assed editing job done while I was about to fall asleep. I'll do better editing later :)

-

My sleep was restless the entire night. Tossing and turning, accommodating for my tied hands. I wake up for about the fifth time, this time to morning sunlight illuminating the curtains from behind.

Right then the door opens, revealing a very worn looking 'Riot Sydney.' His eyes are tired and there's dark purple semicircles beneath them. He looks freshly showered, his wet hair pressed down on his forehead.

His smell makes my wolf howl to the point that I have to take a few breaths to retain myself. A masculine cologne mixes with his natural piney, musky scent, making for my heart to falter a few beats.

He walks over, still refusing to look at me. My spirit drops.

For some reason, I crave his attention. That reason more than likely being the mate bond.

Doesn't he feel it, too?

He holds his palm out towards me.

"Hands," comes the same emotionless command.

I oblige, placing the tied bundle of rope in his open hand. With the other one he starts to cut me free with a single protruded claw on his index finger.

It slices the rope like a razor blade on paper, making me shudder inwardly. The thought of that same claw pressed against flesh, doing that exact same thing, is mortifying.

Once cut, the ropes fall from my wrists. The skin is an angry red, irritated and rubbed raw. The sweat in the abrasions only make it burn worse.

Riot seems to flinch at the sight, his eyes locked intently on my rose colored hands. For a brief moment, I get excited. The look in his eyes— locked anxiously on my hands— almost makes it look like he cares. Like it pains him to see.

When I think he's finally going to say something, he turns away abruptly with a quiet growl and heads for the exit.

And just like that, I'm left alone again.

• • •

Half an hour passes before I finally will myself to wander downstairs. When I do, there's no trace of Riot.

To both my dismay and my pleasure, I find his scent lingering faintly about the house. It triggers a desolate feeling in me. Something unexplainable.

Am I... missing him?

Before I get the chance to figure out what it is, three solid knocks sound from the front door.

At first I freeze, remembering Alpha Andre's latest command: put her back in the cell. Now they've come to get me. They know Riot brought me back and now they know that he's gone.

I take a shaky breath as the icy chill of vulnerability clenches my heart.

A few seconds later, three more knocks come, more impatiently now.

"Goddamn it, open the door, Adrienne!" A very irritated, yet comforting voice yells from the other side. A voice I've got stored away in my memory as belonging to the only friendly person in this pack.

Immediately I'm rushing to the door, my adrenaline-filled fingers fumbling over the handle to get it open.

"Thank the gods you're still alive!" I no more than fling the door open before I'm being pulled into a rib crushing hug.

I inhale Aimee's scent, the familiarity of it a much needed comfort. My nose presses down on the top of her shoulder, my face burrowed into her curly strands of dark brown, almost black hair.

"I swear to you I'll castrate that worthless bastard," she growls, her chin bobbing on my shoulder as she does.

"Have at it," I grumble, finally freeing myself from her suffocating bear hug.

Whether she hears the vexation in my voice or sees it on my face, her brown lips fall into a frown. But it's not a sad frown, because her sharp eyebrows scrunch madly together along with it.

"Where the hell does he get off thinking you owe him a marriage?" Her voice is irate, the more she talks, the angrier she seems to get.

The blackmailed marriage. I had almost completely forgotten about it. And remembering it only makes all of my previous questions resurface. Surely Nathan won't still try to go through with it.

A sickening bile rises in my throat with the thought of how close I came to being bound to that spoiled assbag. The only comfort I find, however, is in the fact that so long as Riot is here, holding the title of Alpha just out of Nathan's reach, then that spoiled brat has no power over me.

"How many died?" Aimee suddenly asks, the burning anger still present in her chocolate colored irises.

I shake my head and shrug. "No idea. Sophia at least."

There's a silent pause between us, not an awkward one, but one long enough to let me sink into my thoughts.

I contemplate telling her about Riot. About my suspicions, about his strange, almost bipolar behavior. But right as the first word is on the tip of my tongue, it falls back down. If I say it out loud, if I allow someone else to know about what I think is between us, then it only becomes that much more real. And that terrifies me.

"How did you know I was here?" I ask instead, changing the subject with a nervous gulp.

She gives me a pointed look. "Adrienne, the entire pack knows he brought you here. That's all they're talking about. How apparently he's using you as some kind of pawn." She rants with disapproval, giving me the impression that Nathan isn't the only one on her shit list.

Although she didn't say a name, only a pronoun, my heart speeds up and my face heats slightly.

Goddamn it, stop.

"Speaking of being a pawn," Aimee continues, oblivious to my spike of nerves, "Andre is asking for you. He's waiting at the pack house."

He's asking for me? After ordering for me to be put back in that hellhole and then sending his son to play a high stakes game of hide and seek with me, he has the audacity to ask for me?

"Tell him he can go fu-"

"You're going," she cuts me off sternly, "And so am I."

• • •

My breath fogs in front of me with every exhale. The air is frigid and dry. The ground remains frozen, a painful reminder of my bleeding, bare feet the previous day.

I pull the door of the pack house open, Aimee's hot breath fanning the back of my neck as I do so.

"Do you want me to come?" She asks gently. I shake my head in response and assure her that I've got it handled. After about a minute of arguing with her, I finally convince her to wait outside.

I walk down the lightless hallway toward the living room. The radiate warmth of a fireplace increases the closer we get.

When we enter, Andre immediately shoots up from the leather couch. His long legs stretch out, no doubt containing pent up energy. His fingers curl repeatedly into strained fists as his livid eyes lock with mine.

He's not pleased. And neither am I.

When he opens his mouth to speak I already anticipate his words.

"I gave you an order and you resisted." He says it in his classic condescending, ashamed tone. The exact tone he uses anytime he wants someone to feel guilty for something that isn't their fault.

I gave you my loyalty and you didn't care, is what I want to say. But for once, as if the silence of the room were giving me time to think, I bite my tongue.

I notice Nathan sitting by the fireplace on an adjacent couch. He cradles his right hand in his lap, and, to my utter shock, he avoids looking up. His head is down and his shoulders are slumped. Just like a newly neutered dog.

"I want to know what's going on between you and that tyrant," he spits the last word through his teeth in disgust. Like it would soil in his mouth if he didn't get it out fast enough.

"W-" I don't get very far in my answer before he cuts me off.

"Tell her what you smelled," he barks at Nathan. For a second I almost think I see the golden boy jump.

"His scent was circling us," Nathan says. It hardly sounds like his voice without the arrogance flowing through it.

So that's why Nathan stopped following me. That's why, for the first time in his privileged life, he gave up on something. It's not because I out-endured him or because he lost my scent or decided to grow a heart and let me go free. It was because Riot's scent was there, threatening him with his presence. Acting like a border between Nathan and I.

I remain silent. I try to keep myself from reading too far into it, but how can I not?

"Don't think this is a permanent thing." As if he read my mind, Andre shatters the bit of hope my wolf instincts had started to drum up.

"Once this problem is dealt with, then he won't be around to intervene with your punishments anymore. Better yet, he won't have a reason to."

His voice is cold. Purposefully indifferent. In fact, it's vain. "Don't get attached, Adrienne. He's not your friend. All you are to him is a pawn."

I don't let a long pause of silence follow his words this time. My jaw has clenched as hard as it possibly can. And if I go any longer without opening it, it'll reach its cracking point.

"And what am I to you?" I snap, staring this shit excuse of an Alpha dead in the eye. For years I looked up to him, admired him even. At one point he was almost like a father to me. But things fucking change, don't they?

"If you say anything other than a pawn or a waste of space, then you're a goddamn liar," I growl. My hands are shaking and my heart is pounding as I dare say my next words. "You should have just left that infant in the rain where you found it."

We play a speechless staring game, Andre and I. He doesn't respond with anger, nor does he wear it on his face. He doesn't have to though. I can feel it filling up the room, ready to swallow us all.

When he finally answers, it's impassive.

"I'll withdraw my order of lock up. For now. You're dismissed."

He doesn't have to say it for me to know to take the truce.

-

I finally updated! Yay!

I'm sorry for this chapter. Truly. It bored the freaking heck out of me just writing it but it had to be done. Hopefully you all haven't given up hope yet, more Riot scenes are coming I promise!

Also, NEW COVER. Yay or nah? Personally it's one of my absolute favorites that I've ever made and I'm obsessed with it.

Thanks for reading!

10 | Something Else

As soon as my feet cross the threshold of the pack house, Aimee is beside me. I expect her to start ranting about Nathan and his father, or badgering me about wanting to know every last word that was said back there.

When she doesn't, I'm shocked.

We get a few meters through the village, walking down the main path between the houses, before she finally opens her mouth.

"Alpha Andre is a controlling, unpleasant, condescending bastard just like his son is."

I breathe out a sigh of relief that she's not gone ill. Here comes the rant I've been anticipating.

"But I do agree with him."

I choke. I physically choke. "You what?!"

"Just hear me out," she holds up her hands, coming to a dead stop in the middle of the pathway and turning to me. She sounds like a peacekeeper now; using that soft, overly reasonable voice to try to cover up the actual meaning of her words.

"The Exiled Alpha is dangerous. It'd be best if you stay away from him. Who knows what the hell he'll do to you," she reasons.

I stare at her blankly, wide eyed and mouth open. I wait for her to start laughing, to elbow me in the ribs and say she's only joking.

But she never does.

It'd be best if you...

That phrase goes right through me. It'd be best if you keep your mouth shut. It'd be best if you'd just do what you're told. It'd be best if you just learn your place.

A hesitant fear crosses Aimee's face and she continues talking with her hands, speaking calmly, "All I'm saying is I've heard things and just... Watch your tongue. The wolf's not stable."

"Do you think it's your turn to move the chess piece?" I accuse hotly, the initial shock subsiding to anger.

Her gaze locks me down on the spot, like a mother getting ready to scold her child.

"Don't be an idiot," she squints at me. "I'm trying not to get you killed. Whatever motives he has, they weren't formulated with the consideration of anyone else."

I don't respond immediately and I find my eyes resting on her, contemplating her perspective.

I don't know his motives. And I don't know his intentions for our pack. There's no argument that I can truthfully use against her here.

As if realizing she's won, her voice softens and quiets.

"You weren't here when he took over Balaige. The rumors we heard were nightmarish. We had no idea if they were true or not, but that only made it worse. And then, nothing. It all stopped," she snaps her fingers, "like that."

She pauses, taking an anxious breath.

"And then we got the word of his exile. You saw the effects of that. The fear," her eyes flit to the ground and back to me, "I'm begging you, Adrienne. Stay away."

Her argument is valid, I'll give her that. Yet I still can't find the fear within me that everyone else has.

I ask, curiously, "What makes him any more dangerous than any other power hungry Alpha?"

She looks around, almost like she's on edge. "He's not of the same breed as the rest of us."

My face scrunches in question. "What do you mean? He's a Lycan?"

"No. The Lycans lived in the same time as the gods and goddesses and died with them as well. But this tyrant, he's something else."

"And what's," I make air quotes using my fingers, "'something else?'"

She shakes her head. "I don't know. I've just heard stories. It's like he's a different breed of werewolf. Something... beyond us."

•••

Aimee and I parted soon after our chat. I left her at the doorstep of her house, not necessarily on bad terms, but tense ones nonetheless. I can see her viewpoint, but somehow it still irritates me and I don't know why.

Now as I climb the steep path winding up one of the mountains surrounding our village, I feel my legs burning. It's not a painful burn though. It's a liberating one.

I come upon a familiar circle of trees, grapevines hanging in thick curtains around them as if to make a wall. Walking up to it, the peacefulness of the place sinks in.

This was my escape. When I still lived in Alpha Andre's house, I would come here to escape Agatha, our housekeeper and nanny. She bore prejudice mindsets, and just like everyone else seems to, she saw me as her target.

She'd pull me away from Nathan and I's training, forcing me instead to clean up their messes. She tried her damnedest to turn me into the perfect maid and housewife. Needless to say, she never succeeded.

When she failed, time after time, she started to resent me because I wouldn't mold to her hands.

"You should have just left that stupid baby to die instead of taking it in. All she's ever caused me is trouble," Agatha's head-splitting voice bitched to Andre one time. Granted, I was eavesdropping; I wasn't suppose to hear it, but it stung then, and it still stings now.

This is where I would come when her nagging became relentless. Where she wouldn't leave me alone even though she hated me. It was the only safe place where she couldn't find me.

Now I need it again.

Pushing a curtain of vines aside, I enter, going straight to the large, flat rock that sits at the other side of the circular outdoor room.

I plop down on it, closing my eyes and resting my head on my folded arms.

Childhood all over again.

I let myself drift off, escaping reality if only for a few minutes. Except I don't get a few. I get about one before all of my senses go into overdrive and my awareness skyrockets.

A presence is standing over me. It takes only a millisecond before my wolf knows exactly who it is.

I pop one eye open and look up at him. He's expressionless— as always— but there's something in his eyes. Something like... sympathy?

"Come on," his deep, stone-like voice speaks.

I heave out a long sigh. All I want is sleep. But apparently that's asking too much. Though at the same time, I'm too tired to put up a fight.

I sit up on the rock, the top of my head coming up level to the bottom of Riot's chest.

"Where are we- hey!"

One of his arms scoops up my legs whilst the other snakes around my torso before lifting my bottom off the rock completely.

As soon as the side of my body presses against him, my muscles turn to jelly.

Goddamn whatever this feeling is.

Just like before, when he carried me into the Alpha's house, I'm lulled into a state of dopey tranquility. In that moment I give up, leaving myself both figuratively and literally in Riot's hands.

The last thing I see before shutting my eyes and resting my head on his solid shoulder, is the vines being pushed aside as he carries us through them.

•••

The ride ends all too soon when we come up on a large cabin nestled between the trees. I blink the sleep from my eyes and try to get a better look.

The sides are varnished and clean, along with many crystal clear windows. He walks up the steps and onto the porch, his shoes tapping against the wood.

My feet meet with the ground when he all but tosses me down, taking the pleasant feeling away like cold water dumped over my head. I stumble slightly before finding my balance. I catch a growl in my throat before it can escape.

He's already turned away from me, facing the door. His body blocks sight of whatever he's doing, but I can hear the mechanical sound of a lock twisting.

Suddenly I remember Aimee's fear. I can hear the shake of her voice and see her wide, serious eyes. She wouldn't lie to me, nor would she have a motive to. All she wants is for me to survive.

I think about running. Now could be the last chance I get before I go into that house where he intends to do god knows what to me.

Mate. The word comes to mind along with a deafening pulse, like there's water in my ears.

My wolf gravitates towards him, wanting nothing but to lean into him and feel the electric touch once again.

Common sense, however, pulls me the other way.

In a spilt second, half-assed decision, I find myself leaping over the railing and pumping my legs as fast as they can go. I know I've made a mistake when a monstrous snarl shakes the ground beneath me.

I sprint deeper into the forest, the shadows growing darker the further I go. The will to survive encourages me to keep moving, my blood pumping faster. A minute passes by, maybe two, but in reality it's only been a couple of seconds.

Then, without a warning, something heavier than a boulder barrels into me. I crumple to the ground from the impact with its weight crushing my lungs. I gasp for air, claws digging into my shoulder blades as large paws hold me firmly against the ground to make sure I don't get up again.

I swallow hard, gathering enough words to speak.

"I won't run anymore," I say, breathing heavily both from the adrenaline and the short game of predator and prey.

He growls in approval and steps off of me, although still standing over me. With one paw he rolls me over onto my back, and sure enough, that same enormous wolf I remember is towering over me with searing eyes.

You've screwed up now, Adrienne.

He snatches my shirt collar between his teeth, pulling me to my feet as he back-steps. I don't object, realizing that it's probably in my best interest to do things that discourage him from moving those canines an inch over and sticking them into my throat.

He guides me back to the cabin, his muzzle never far from my neck, ready to grab me again any second.

This is the second time I've been shoved at snout-point back to a place I tried to escape from. Maybe this whole escapee thing isn't my cup of tea after all. Or maybe I just need new tactics.

"I'm going," I grumble as he prods his nose into the small of my back, urging me through the doorway of the cabin.

I'm pushed up a flight of polished wooden stairs, down a dark hallway, and into a bedroom. Riot doesn't follow me into it.

On my own accord, I go to sit on the edge of the immaculately white comforter spread across the bed.

My mind races, trying to make up some kind of logical reason as to why he's brought me here. Away from my pack; the pack he's just conquered.

Movement in the corner of my eye grabs my attention. Riot, standing on two legs now, enters. Dread fills me up as I spot what's he's bringing with him.

"Hands," comes that same emotionless, I-couldn't-care-less command.

I oblige, tiredly. He ties them up tightly, just as before.

"Ass," I murmur, glaring at his fingers as they pull the knot tighter. He doesn't acknowledge my insult.

Without a word this time, he walks over the doorway, flips the lights into darkness, and closes the door behind him. My new bedtime ritual.

-

Thoughts on the chapter?

Do you agree with Aimee about her precautions about the Exiled Alpha?

Why do you think Riot took Adrienne from Visari territory and to a completely isolated cabin?

Thanks for reading!

11 | You're Bipolar

All through the night, there were strange sounds outside my door. Footsteps would often pace back and forth in the hallway, accompanied by canine sounds. Sometimes low and inconsistent growling, sometimes indistinct snarls, and other times quiet whimpering.

One time there was scratching on the walls. It was in short and frenzied strokes, no doubt tearing all the way into the insulation.

On multiple occasions the doorknob would jiggle, like something was holding it from the other side. But it never did open. The pressure would let up after a minute or so. Then all of the sounds would leave until they returned a couple of hours later in a different, unprecedented pattern.

I wake up for about the fourth time, this time to morning sunlight illuminating the curtains from behind.

My stomach voices its dissatisfaction with a long, drawn out gurgle. The empty feeling in it is torturous.

Either it's my cruel imagination hoping to taunt me, or I smell food cooking. The sweet aroma of French toast in particular.

As if on cue, the doorknob twists and swings open, making me jump out of my skin. Riot strides straight towards me, making my heart thumb out of control.

He looks miserable. Disheveled reddish brown hair, dark semicircles tainting the skin beneath his eyes. His broad shoulders, usually held high, are slouching and his mouth is pressed into a thin, emotionless line.

Avoiding my eyes with his own, he holds out a large open palm to me. "Hands."

With the razor blades at the ends of his fingers, he cuts the ropes off. The red, irritated, burning skin hurts and looks just as bad as last time, if not worse.

"Food's downstairs if you want it," He says before exiting the room, this time leaving the door open behind him.

• • •

Mate.

That's a funny concept.

I've heard so many stories of what a mate is suppose to be. How everything is suppose to be perfect and taken straight from a story book.

Maybe I'm just being skeptical-- hell, that's exactly what I am, but this is far from what everyone promised. One moment he acts like he cares, cleaning my wounds so gently, and then the next I'm being tied up like a dog.

Nonetheless, I couldn't pass up the offer of food. I lingered a bit in the room before going after him. When I stepped out of the room, the hallway was found in a mess. There were places on the carpet that were shredded to threads. Long claw marks were carved messily into the wall, fluffy pink material leaking out. A chill went down my spine at the sight before turning away.

My nose acted as a guide as I made my way down the stairs following the sweet aromas. It lead me to the kitchen, golden sunlight spilling in through the sliding glass door and the window above the sink.

I walk in just as Riot is sitting a plate filled with food on a wooden framed glass table. He barely glances at me before leaving the room.

What the hell is wrong with this guy?

Huffing to voice my annoyance, I ignore the strange behavior and sit down in front of the plate, not hesitating to start eating. My eyes widen at the burst of flavor.

I don't bother taking my attention from the syrupy goodness, not even when hearing him re-enter the room. I sense his presence move to the opposite end of the table, sitting down across from me.

The only sound besides the silence is my fork occasionally tinging against the plate. When I get ready to cut off another bite, I feel him staring at my hands.

"They'll heal," I reassure him. Once I speak he finally gives me the eye contact my wolf has long been demanding.

He nods his head, his eyes refusing to leave mine. In that instance he looks somewhat vulnerable, like a child after they were caught doing something they shouldn't be. It makes me want to leap across the table and hug him, telling him over and over again that I'll be alright.

Eventually I look away and down at my food, but feel too uncomfortable to eat now.

I don't know what the future holds, whether I'm expected to live here with him or not. Or am I just his hostage? Maybe he planned to use me for ransom. That would make sense as to why he cared so much about what I meant to Nathan: the closer we are, the bigger the reward.

But yet again, that same controversial word comes to mind.

Mate.

There's no doubt about it. Riot and I are mates. Will he accept that though? So far, he's doing a shit poor job at it.

"Why won't you tell me your name?"

I look up again to study him. There's a sort of desperation on his expression, emphasized by the dark circles on either side of the bridge of his nose.

He couldn't have gotten much sleep last night. Judging by the restless sounds that were outside my door and the condition of the hall, he went through a torture beyond imaginable.

I lay my fork down. "The same reason you don't reward a dog with a treat for a trick he hasn't done."

If he wants to tie me up like an animal, then two can play at that game.

The familiar rumbling starts in his chest again and his fingers turn white as they grip the edge of the table.

"You're weird," he mumbles whilst studying me suspiciously at an angle.

He's calling me weird? The one who went out of his way to invade my pack and drag me away to an unfamiliar forest is acting as if I'm the pest?

"You're bipolar," I retort, leaning back in my chair and crossing my arms to watch him with the same skeptical gaze he's sending my way.

Seconds turn into minutes, and minutes into hours as we sit there in an unspoken staring context. The longer he stares at me the louder my heartbeat sounds in my ears. The longer I stare at him the more I want to feel the touch of his skin on mine.

He starts to squirm slightly in his chair, in visible discomfort.

He breaks first.

A grin cracks my lips when he pushes his chair back harshly as he stands up, growling to himself. My head turns with him as he walks over to the glass door leading to the outside.

"Come on." He slides it open and steps outside, stopping and looking back to make sure I'm coming.

Slowly, I rise to my feet, following him out the door and sliding it closed behind me. "Where are we going?" I question, on high alert once again.

He begins walking straight into the woods, which isn't surprising since the cabin is in the middle of a forest.

"I need to let my wolf out and if I leave you alone you'd run away." He doesn't pay attention to me as he answers, looking straight ahead as if I'm not even there.

He needs to let his wolf out? That must have been what all the commotion was last night. His wolf is restless and by fighting it he's only tormenting himself.

"Riot," I say. He falters on one step but quickly covers it up, like he almost stopped in his tracks but didn't. He looks over at me as if to ask a silent 'what?'

"Oh nothing," I continue nonchalantly, facing forward apathetically, "I was just seeing how it felt to say my mate's name. How does it feel, Riot?"

It occurs to me that that's the first time I've openly acknowledged the mate bond between us. It's not like it's a secret because he has to feel it too, but still, something about it feels risqué. Maybe it's because he ignores all of the mutual sensations that I know he feels. Or maybe it's because I'm just a hostage he's waiting for the right chance to get rid of.

I glance over at him out of the corner of my eye. He comes to a dead stop, a clawed hand swinging up to stick into a nearby tree. His form is shaking almost violently. His beautiful copper eyes have darkened tenfold, all the way back to the obsidian color I've grown used to.

"Tell me. Your name," He orders with a clipped tone, his voice distorted in a snarl.

I pause for a minute, thinking carefully. He's always had a sort of baleful aura about him. But this, this is on a new level. A level that could— would— be potentially life threatening.

"No."

He suddenly doubles over in a fashion that I've seen way too much. He's losing control, and it's only a matter of seconds before his body morphs into that of a wolf's— a seething one at that.

I don't stick around to witness the shifting. My feet are pounding against the ground in the opposite direction as soon as my brain processes what's happening— and registers the fact that I caused it.

A wolf is easily faster than a human. A human sprinting at full speed still wouldn't stand a chance against a wolf just jogging. Four legs are better than two, I guess. With that in mind, I shift into my own wolf without even slowing down.

The wind blows through my cream colored fur, blessing every hair with a cool caress. My paws thud against the ground rhythmically, the crisp air circulating through my lungs.

This is what freedom feels like.

Excluding the fact that a seething, irate beast is sure to be on my trail, it feels liberating. Nathan never understood that, not even when we were friends. He thought my morning runs through the mountains were silly. A waste of time even. He never did understand. But I guess when your parents serve everything to you on a golden platter, the small things become irrelevant.

The frantic and multiplied flapping of wings overhead makes me trot to a stop. Crows are fleeing in abundance from the direction I'm heading in, cawing their shrill warnings as they go back the way I came.

I look around the unfamiliar setting, searching for whatever could have scared them. The brush is so thick in this area of the forest that anything could be hiding in the growth.

My ears perk at the sharp snap of a stick ahead. Instantly my eyes land on a figure standing among the undergrowth.

"Adrienne?"

-

Thank you so much for reading! Don't be afraid to leave your thoughts in a comment, I love reading them.

12 | Bad Ideas

"Adrienne?" I recognize the Alpha-to-be, Nathan, approaching me. "Where the hell have you been?! Here," he takes his jacket off and tosses it at me.

"Shift back."

He says it so demandingly, and with a pang of irritation in his voice. As if he's actually angry with me for making him go through the trouble to find me. Like it was my fault the tyrant picked me to carry off into the woods.

I glare at the jacket in disgust: the same way I look at him.

As repulsive as the idea of wearing his clothes is, I don't have much of a choice. I have to find out what he and his father are planning, and to do that, I'd have to speak.

After taking the jacket in my teeth, I glower at him pointedly until he takes the hint and turns around. The familiar sensation of my bones breaking, reshaping, then fusing back together overtakes my body. In the matter of a couple seconds, I'm standing on two legs again, my windblown blonde hair hanging down to brush the small of my back.

The sound of the zipper signals for Nathan to turn back around. I have to bend and pull at the jacket to get it to reach far enough to cover everything, leaving me in an awkward half-standing, half-crouching position.

"Problem?" He asks with a dumb smirk on his face. He, at least, has the luxury of pants.

"Looking at it," I snap without hesitation, making a point by staring him dead in the eye.

He growls, his cocky mood suddenly changing to one of vexation.

"Don't even give me your fucking attitude. Get your ass over here so we can go. The wedding was rescheduled to three days from now and I can't stand up there alone." His expression suddenly darkens, becoming more frighteningly seriously.

My jaw drops. After all that's happened, and he's still pushing this?

I notice him progressively coming closer, but at a slow pace, reminding me of a snake watching its prey. "I was promised certain things, Adrienne. And I fully expect to get those things."

My skin starts to crawl with the thought of whatever "things" could be running through his sick head.

"I already told you, there's not gonna be a wedding," I growl out, a shadow overlaying my own irises now.

He smiles, a devious gleam in his eye. "And my father already told you what would happen if you didn't. I wouldn't be able to visit you down there— nobody would."

My stomach drops at his words. I had forgotten about that threat until now. There truly isn't any winning scenario to choose from. One way I'm being forced into a depraved marriage, and the other I'd be stuck with a psyched out mate who may only want to sell me back to my pack for ransom. And then I'd be back to square one.

Nathan is just a few yards from me, making me tense with vulnerability. On normal circumstances, it wouldn't be an issue. As kids we went through the exact same training, learning and exploiting each other's weaknesses. But now, one wrong move and I'll be the equivalent of naked.

Right as I begin to feel panic set in, we both jump at the sound of a snarl so powerful that it shakes the ground beneath our feet.

Nathan is frozen in place, his eyes the size of saucers. For a second I think he's gaping at me, until I realize that he's looking over my shoulder.

Riot is behind me. His claws carve deep marks into the trees as he stalks past them, dragging his flexed fingertips over the bark as he goes. Large canines hide behind his parted lips, sharp enough to rip the flesh off bone with barely a graze.

His black eyes glow a deep ruby red, the same color I remember leaping from the woods the night of the ceremony. There's something threatening about them, something haunting. I can't help but to sense one crucial thing about them, and it's that those are the eyes of the wolf inside him.

A shiver goes down my spine when they land on me. More particularly, the jacket around me.

I want to say something but the words are jumbled in my throat. Before I can blink, my back is being thrown against the ground, a large figure on top me.

The fabric screams as he rips it at the seams. His long claws frantically shred it into pieces until there's nothing left to cover my shame, leaving me feeling cold and exposed.

My arms come up to cover my chest while I cross my legs to hide what little they can.

I hastily curl into a ball by habit, shielding my abdomen from view more than anything. Covering my stomach is still second nature to me, despite my private parts being subject to the same jeopardy.

I timidly look up to see Riot standing over me. In one swift motion he pulls his shirt over his head, dropping it carelessly on top of me.

As he stretched his arms over his head, his body seemed to tell a story. The further the shirt went, the more things it revealed on his smooth skin. Three long scars ran diagonally across his left pec in the form of a claw mark. Despite those flaws, he's sculpted better than a Greek statue; well defined muscles gliding beneath his skin with every movement.

Realizing a drop of saliva forming in the corner of my mouth, I tear my eyes away.

Stupid mate bond.

Without a second thought I cling onto the shirt for dear life. It's not exactly a full outfit, but it's better than nothing.

I brace myself to find those petrifying yet stunning eyes burning into mine, but Riot doesn't have any further interest in me. Instead his attention falls on Nathan.

He moves ever so slowly in his direction, like a lion tormenting it's prey just for the fun of it. Except there's nothing close to fun about him. Anger rolls off of his body in thick waves, enough to make anyone's nerves crack, even daddy's spoiled little brat.

Nathan's face is pale, just like it was the last time I saw him. Every step Riot takes forward, is another step Nathan takes back. He eventually realizes that there's no where to go. The initial state of terror must have worn off, because his attitude changes just like the wind.

"You're the bastard who crashed my party. Tried to take my pack," Nathan growls, that vein in his neck starting to twitch. Something that has become far too familiar to me.

He pauses, glancing past Riot and at me before back to his active threat. "I want her back. I'll pay whatever your price is, but she comes with me."

And then, just as all of his conversations go halfway through, the polite tone in his voice drops. It sours into one of mockery, "I get that it must get lonely in exile, but find your own Luna. This one's taken."

It seems as if the whole world goes quiet, waiting for what's to come. I breath in, my heart pounding in my ears.

The calm before the storm.

Riot goes rigid.

Nathan's face falls.

Then the storm breaks loose.

A feral snarl tears from his throat, making me jolt with the natural instinct of danger. But I'm not the one who has to worry about that.

In the blink of an eye, there's blood spraying from Nathan's nose, Riot's knuckles having busted the dam. His neck turns at an unnatural angle and a loud, echoing pop makes me cringe back. But it doesn't end there. Riot continues throwing punch after punch, even after he's straddling him on the ground. Nathan struggles beneath him, in the end eating more fists than he deflects.

I notice the spine rising along Riot back, pushing up against the skin as it forms a bumpy ridge. A telltale sign of the shifting to come.

A jolt of electricity shoots through me, alarms going off at the sight. I've seen him as a wolf before, but he only had black irises then. He was in control for the most part. The red glow to them, however, means something entirely different. Something that I don't want to witness.

"RIOT!!!" The scream comes out before I can stop it, so unexpected that my voice breaks halfway through.

Maybe my wolf knows something I don't, because what I saw as pointless screaming made him stop dead. His fist comes to a sudden halt halfway to Nathan's face.

Riot's head snaps to look at me, on full alert. His wild eyes flicker, as if scanning for more enemies. Then, as if realizing what he's doing, he glances down at his victim, then back to me.

He comes towards me at a quickened pace, scooping me up off the ground without even slowing down. He cradles me like he did before, looking straight ahead and acting like he doesn't feel the sparks between us.

As I'm carried away with long strides, heart thumping against my sternum, I try peaking over Riot's shoulder.

Is he...?

A thunderous growl sounds out and Riot drops him arms down, lowering me so that I can't see past him.

His bare chest is warm and inviting. I find myself unconsciously nestling into him, my wolf starving for the sense of safety being near him gives me.

His scars are right beside my face now, peaking my curiosity. Gently, I begin tracing them with my finger, feeling the contour of the damaged tissue.

His body tenses at my touch, yet he refuses to acknowledge it. His jaw clenches tightly, stifling a reaction.

In an act of mercy, I drop my hand into my lap. Pushing his wolf again isn't a good idea. In fact, it's terrible one. Nathan might've learned the hard way, but I certainly don't need to.

Letting out a small sigh, I lay my head on his collarbone.

"It's Adrienne Gage."

He cranes his neck, and even though I can't see his face, I know he's looking down at me.

"What?"

"My name," I clarify, mindlessly studying the curves of his bicep. "It's Adrienne Gage."

-

Oooh is anyone starting to warm up to Riot now? Her telling him her name is one of if not my absolute favorite scene in this book.

Thank you for reading!

13 | Are You Jealous?

I had started to fall asleep in Riot's arms. My eyelids began batting slowly until they closed. Barely awake, I feel him squeeze me closer to his body. The electricity between our skin lulls me into tranquility.

Except this time reality doesn't come back like a slap to the face. He doesn't drop me as soon as we get to the cabin like last time. He carries us through the door, up the stairs, and down the hall further than I've been before. He turns into another bedroom, this one with black walls and white trim, basically the opposite of the one I'd slept in.

He sits me down in the middle of the room, the plush carpet soft against my bare feet. He starts rummaging through dressers, plucking out articles of clothing.

Soon he walks over to a door on the far side of the room, opening it. He holds out the handful of clothes to me as I approach.

"Everything should be in there."

With that he all but shoves the clothes against my chest, walking out of the room.

His latest nice streak is now over. But at least it lasted longer that the previous ones.

I step into the bathroom and lock the door behind me. Undressing is simple since the only thing I had to cover me was his shirt.

I lay the clothes he'd given me on the counter after quickly looking through them. A black v-neck and grey sweatpants, both which smell like him.

• • •

Riot didn't talk for the rest of the day, which left me on my own. And of course, leaving wasn't an option. While I spent most of my time playing solitaire with a deck of cards I'd found, he was pacing around the house, restless. A lot of the time he was outside, just watching the woods. I suspected Nathan had put him on edge and he probably expected him to send more wolves after us.

I'd made the living room my home for the day. It has a typical hunting lodge feel to it. There's high windows that fill it with natural light and various animal mountings, the main spectacle being an enormous moose head hanging above the grand stone fireplace. The floors are wooden, stained with a dark varnish to perfect the look.

Despite the beautiful room, there was something strange about it. All of the furniture was wrapped in plastic, as if to keep the dust off of it. This made my mind reel. Was the house abandoned and he just found it? Or was it his and he only used it on special occasions, such as a kidnapping? I had uncovered part of the large leather couch, allowing enough room to let me sit comfortably, sinking down into it.

As I reach forward to move another card on the coffee table, the same words go through my head for the millionth time. "Tried to take my pack... It must be lonely in exile."

I haven't been able to get my mind off of it.

Exile. A word I'd heard all too often lately.

As if on cue, the door opens and closes, signaling that Riot is back. He'll stay for roughly an hour, and then he would leave again. That's the pattern he's following all day.

I feel his presence moving across the room behind the couch, ignoring my existence like it's nothing. It bothers me. It makes my chest crawl with a fear I want so badly to forget the feeling of. I haven't said anything to him being brought back here. And I don't want the chance to be voiceless again. Not to him.

"You wanna play?" I ask, anxiety pooling in my belly along with anticipation, "I'm tired of beating myself."

I wait a couple seconds, hopeful, but he keeps walking. The saliva in my mouth goes cold.

No... No, it's fine. He's not ignoring me... he's... he's thinking of an answer. It's fine.

When no reaction comes, I try again, "Afraid of losing? I guess I can understand that." The panic grows by the millisecond. My hands are jittery as I reach out to pick up another card, trying to convince myself to be casual.

He's almost gone now, one foot out of the room.

He doesn't hear me. He's not turning around.

At the last minute, in a flash of desperation, I blurt out his name, almost yelling, "Riot."

He stops, standing in the doorway with his back to me.

"Why am I here?" I ask, the silence of the room amplifying, "If I'm such a damn bother to you then just let me leave." The more I talk the angrier I get. I was brought here against my will only for the one whose suppose to be my mate to act like I'm a nuisance he was stuck with.

He turns around slowly. I flinch when his dark eyes are staring daggers at me.

There's so much venom in his voice that I have to hold back a whimper—another doing of the mate bond.

"Why? So you can go back to him? Good luck picking him off ground," he ends in a growl, his hands flexing like the first time I saw him.

He wants to hit something, or fight someone. Anything that lets his aggression be released.

My brow furrows tightly, and going against all my instincts, I raise my voice at him, "What the hell are you talking about?"

I jump back at the sudden shattering of glass, the arm of the couch jutting into my back. I quickly spot the fragmented vase pieces strewn across the floor.

Or throw something. That works, too.

"Tell me you're not his Luna." He's shaking as he comes closer, but his voice is as steady as a kill shot, deadly and certain.

The length of the couch is the only thing separating us now, and even that's not enough. I can feel the presence of his wolf surfacing, the same lethal aura that rolled off of him before Nathan got in his way.

The fear starts to disintegrate. That's what was bothering him? That's what made him hate me for the entire day?

My stomach flutters with excitement at the thought of him being possessive. One word could send him off the edge at this point. It'd be like throwing a bone off the cliff and watching his wolf drag him off after it. So I say four.

"Why? Are you jealous?" An amused smirk curls my lips.

"Fucking right I am," he responds immediately, with dead certainty.

I blink, the smirk falling from my face, "Wait... what...?"

Him admitting to caring about me was the last thing I expected.

He steps closer, the couch proving to be a sad excuse of a barrier. My back arches, the arm rest preventing me from scooting away any further.

Soon he's right in front of me, barely giving me room to breath. His arms cage me, one on the arm rest and one on the back of the couch. The close proximity hits me like a punch in the gut, forcing all the air out of my lungs. When I inhale again, my nose fills with his addictive scent.

I swallow, trying not to let the regret show on my face.

"Answer me." His face is unreadable, but his voice is a death warning.

I give what sounds like more of a question than an answer. "Um... Techn ically...?"

A growl rips from his throat, deafening and murderous. The leather squeals as it tears at the mercy of his claws. I press myself even further into the cushions, wishing it would just have mercy and finish swallowing me whole.

"You know this couch looks really expensive and I'm not gonna be the one to pay for it to get reupholstered so-"

"Did he touch you?" He asks through clenched canines, cutting off my nervous rambling. His mouth opens and closes again, like he wants to say something else but stops himself.

My unfocused gaze falls to his chest. "No."

He leans in closer, the tip of his nose caressing my jaw as he inhales the scent on my skin. His voice is so low and soft that it sends ice through my veins, making me shiver.

"Now he never will."

My fingertips ache with the need to touch him. To feel his body flush against mine in a solid embrace. I itch to watch his muscles flex beneath his tanned skin and to study his scar further. The collar of his shirt only teases me, gravity pulling it down as he's bent over me, giving me just a small glimpse.

His eyes, which have turned an impossible shade darker, roam over every inch of my face. My forehead, my cheekbones, and my nose, until eventually landing on my lips.

His mouth is slightly parted, his tongue unconsciously flicking out to wet his own lips.

Cautiously, I reach my hand up to curl my fingers gently around his wrist. When he doesn't pull away, I begin running my hand slowly up his arm, feeling the exquisite raises and dips of his muscles.

A rumbling, yet soft sound is coming from him, like a canine purr. By the time my palm reaches his shoulder, he seems to lean in closer.

My fantasy cuts off before it can even start when he suddenly moves away, standing up straight. The sight of his receding form is like a bucket of cold water over my head.

He's heading for the door, but I don't want him to leave. Not now.

"He wants me to marry him," I say off the top of my head. He stops in his tracks, every muscle in his body visibly contracting. A human might not be able to notice the small things, but a werewolf definitely can. And the sound of his knuckles cracking makes me tense.

"His father arranged it. I wouldn't have had a choice. The party that you... crashed... that was the bonding ceremony." When I stop talking I feel like I could drown in the silence that's so thick in the air.

There's no growl. No snarl. No nothing.

"Riot?"

He flinches slightly at the sound of his name. Then he shakes his head and continues walking out of the room.

Just like that, I'm unheard again. It feels like my heart shrivels in my chest. I've always envisioned it wilting like a flower. But this time it feels worse. So much worse.

With one last glance towards the cards laid out on the table, I lay down, burying my face against the cool leather.

-

Things are getting more intense. But is it for the best or the worst? Share your thoughts :)

Thanks for reading!

14 | Going Too Far

W hen I wake up, the room is dark, lit dimly by the light of the fireplace. I sit up with a soft groan, rubbing the sleep from my eyes.

The first thing I notice is the plastic removed from all the furniture. The second thing is the aroma of tomato sauce in the air. And the third is Riot sitting on the other end of the couch, watching me intently.

"Food?" I murmur, the heel of my hand still pressed against my eye.

He leans forward to grab something off the coffee table and presents me with a steaming plate of spaghetti. It's warm to the touch and I take it graciously.

Curling the noodles around my fork, I try to brush off the feeling of his eyes on me. Expecting him to talk is far from realistic. So I don't bother getting my hopes up.

A few minutes pass by, my chewing uncomfortably loud in the otherwise quiet room. Finally, I can't take it anymore.

"Riot?" I ask, looking up from my plate.

"Hm?"

"Who are you?" I know who he is. The entire pack constantly whispering and talking about him made sure of that. But somehow it seems surreal. So surreal in fact, that I need it to come from his lips instead of a jittery pack member.

There's a pause, only seeming to confirm my answer past what words could.

"I think you know." His expression doesn't change, but his eyes let something slip. There's a flash of something, there and gone in half a second.

I swallow. The soft sound of metal tings as I drop my fork on the plate.

My voice is barely above a whisper, like I'm half afraid of what will happen at saying the title, "You're the Exiled Alpha."

Another pause. I lose my appetite.

"Yes."

This is who everyone has been making a fuss over. The one they shake in their own skin at just the thought of. This wolf in front of me is a single tyrant who has made every Alpha fear for their position ever since word of his exile got out.

Something within me didn't want to believe that before. It's almost as if, subconsciously, I had dismissed everyone's talk of being nothing more than rumors.

But rumors don't sit in front of you and agree with you.

"Eat," he urges, noticing how I'm staring blankly at my food.

I shake my head, "I'm not hungry."

I uncross my legs and get up from the couch, taking my plate and an empty one from the coffee table, presumably his. When I walk past him I avert his gaze, keeping mine to the ground.

This shouldn't change anything. Knowing who he is and accepting it should only deepen my understanding of him. But it doesn't. It only complicates what already has my head in a mess.

What wouldn't sink in before now starts to. The fact that this infamous figurehead has taken me captive and refuses to feel the bond between us. It's unreal. It's... frustrating.

Suddenly I whirl back around, sitting the plates down on a nearby stand as I do so.

"Why are you resisting?" There's heat to my words, all of the pent up frustration leaking out, "I know you feel it, so why are you fighting it? Am I really that goddamn terrible?"

His fingers tighten on the couch, balling the leather into his fist. When he answers, it's grudging and through clenched teeth, "Just drop it."

My expression sours, contemplating for a minute. "No."

I stare hard, making sure that he feels the scrutiny burning into his skull.

"Tell me why you were outside my door all night," I demand, crossing my arms and shifting my weight, "Answer me that and I'll never ask anything ever again."

"You're going too far," he grits out, repressing a growl.

"I have a guess," I continue pushing him, "You're trying to fight what your wolf-"

"Adrienne," he warns with a deathly undertone, "Stop."

The sound of my name off his tongue for the first time makes my heart accelerate, threatening or not.

In a split and thoughtless second, I spit back a taunting response. "That's funny. Nathan has never asked me to stop."

The words are out before I can stop them. It doesn't take me long to realize the weight of what I've just said. Or to feel my body pulse with panic as regret sets in.

My arms fall to my sides, as does the smug look on my face when the house shakes with a thunderous roar. I cover my ears and close my eyes, but I still hear the loud, banging racket.

When I look again the couch is flipped over on its backside and laying on the complete opposite side of the room. Riot is facing me, his chest heaving rapidly as a constant growl comes from his throat. The deep ruby glow of his blackened irises in the dark put the light of the fire to shame.

He takes a hesitant step towards me, then two steps back before abruptly turning and striding for the front door. My feet are glued to the floor as I watch him swing it open. It slams into the wall with enough force to undoubtedly form a hole.

It seems like an eternity before I can snap myself out of my daze.

What have I done?

I jog out onto the porch after him, just in time to catch the view of an enormous dark furred wolf disappearing into the forest.

I don't expect him to come back, not anytime soon. He needs space, so I try to wait. I try to pass time faster with sheer force of will and want. Which only turns into me prancing restlessly around the house.

What if he's going after Nathan— assuming he's even alive— to finish what he started? Or what if he's just leaving me here with no sense of navigation to the way back to my pack? Or maybe he just wants away from me. If it's the latter, then I can't say I blame him.

Telling my overly-aggressive mate that I had relations with a wolf he already hated. That's sure to get him to open up.

Enough time passes for my stomach to knot up with guilt. Every passing minute I'm coming up with scenarios of what he could be doing out there, each one worse than the last. Eventually I can't take it anymore and find myself wandering amidst the looming trees. Following the distinctive scent of Riot Sydney.

The moon shines harshly overhead, but even its light can't penetrate the thick canopy of leaves. There's a gentle yet chilling wind blowing through my hair, disheveling it.

I start to wonder why I'm out here. Why I'm not running to find the way back to my pack. Why, instead, I'm tracking down the infamous Alpha in exile whose title has the world shaking in paranoia.

"Adrienne," I melt at his voice, coming somewhere from the shadows. I turn in its direction.

Riot is sitting slumped against a tree, his fingers tangled tightly in his hair. He doesn't bother to hide his nudity. It takes one glance before I'm averting my gaze, heat rushing to my cheeks.

"I don't know what you want me to say."

He's staring aimlessly at the ground, his elbow propped on his knee. He looks exhausted, his eyelids and lips drooping.

My brow furrows. "What do you mean?"

His hand drops from his hair and he laughs bitterly. "I don't fucking know. It's like, when you're around all my senses go into overdrive. When you're close, my heart starts pounding harder and I can't think straight because my wolf goes dumb in the head and I always wanna touch you and it's fucking weird."

He says it all in minimal breaths, the words rushing out. His tone is sharp, fluctuating between high and low notes.

I take a step forward. The sight of him hurting hurts me in turn.

"Please don't," he begs, dragging his palm over his face.

"Riot-"

"God, don't say my name."

"Why?" I challenge, defying him by easing closer, "Because you're afraid you'll feel something?"

"I'm not afraid," he snaps.

The wind blows in his direction, moving my hair to lay on my chest. His nostrils flare, and I know he can smell my scent.

"Then show me," I say, taking another bold step, "Show me that you're not afraid."

He throws his head back suddenly, letting out a deep, guttural sound. His lips curl back in a wince, revealing sharpened teeth.

He's clashing with his wolf again, this time in a losing battle.

In a flash I'm to him, kneeling at his side. Somehow I stay calm despite the apprehension growing within me.

"You don't have to fight it." I resist the urge to throw myself at him or to even touch him. I don't know how he would react to that, especially in a state as distressed as this.

His chin lowers back down until his eyes meet mine. There's a brokenness in them that makes my heart ache, that makes an all too familiar pang of hatred ricochet on the walls of my stomach.

His voice is quiet and defeated, "I want to touch you. I want to touch you so bad."

Gingerly, I hold out my hand, "So touch me."

He inspects it for a few seconds, as if deciding whether to trust me or not. With great caution, his hand raises to engulf mine, our fingers lacing like a perfect puzzle piece. He watches our hands intently, like he's actually trying to see the invisible sparks dancing between our skin.

I break the hold, and in the time that our contact is broken, a flash of panic crosses his face. Like he's afraid of losing something.

My fingers wrap around his wrist, bringing his palm up to cup my cheek.

"It's okay," I whisper reassuringly. His fingers twitch at the touch before giving my face a gentle squeeze.

"We need to get back to the cabin," I say, searching his face and failing to make out an emotion.

"Why?" His posture suddenly improves, alert eyes darting around the forest around us.

I stand up, pulling him up with me, "Because the couch is in the wall and I don't clean up messes that aren't mine."

I love this little scene between Riot and Adrienne. I think it sort of shows a bit more of them from the inside.

Please share your thoughts!

Thank you for reading!

15 | A Different Breed

Riot lingers claustrophobically behind me as I lead the way back to the cabin. He isn't touching me, except for his hot breath tickling my shoulder. I bite my tongue.

He's not stable. He's been struggling far worse than what I realized. If I want him to trust me, then I'm sure as hell not going to push him away.

We walk through the front door that was left slammed open. He frowns when his eyes land on the couch. One end is propped in the wall, drywall powder dusting it white.

"We'll worry about it later," I say, going around him to jerk the door handle out of yet another hole in the wall. I shut it and lock it. "You should sleep."

I take in his weary appearance. The circles are still under his eyes, the whites of which look bloodshot and glassy at best. His coppery hair is messier than usual, going in all directions and teased by rough fingers running through it too frequently.

He looks like shit, but somehow, he still manages to look more attractive than any other being. It irks me.

I half expect him to argue, but instead he nods tiredly. I take his wrist and lead him up the stairs without any complaints. Once in his room, I walk him over to the bed. As soon as he sits down I go to the dressers, rummaging through them.

I return to his side, holding out a pair of boxers and dark grey sweatpants. While I wait for him to take them I keep my vision busy in a hardcore stare on the furthest wall.

"I couldn't find the shirts. Hope this is okay," I say, trying anything to get rid of the awkward silence.

He mumbles a quick 'it's fine,' before he takes the clothes and stands up. I turn my back to him as he puts them on. The bed dips softly, signaling for me to look again.

He's laying face down in the pillow, his elbows sprawled out to the sides. His back is sculpted just like the rest of his body: defined shoulder blades and prominent muscles.

My roaming eyes stop dead when they land on a point of interest— a black insignia burned into the base of his neck. The ink depicts the head of a snarling dire wolf: the symbol of the packless.

Centuries ago, even in primal times, wolves kept to packs— the same packs which are still alive today. But there were some wolves, feral ones, who didn't. They were dire wolves, said to have different genetics than the rest of us. A different supernatural breed of werewolf.

As society evolved, the dires were looked down upon. They were feared because they were wild and savage, so they started being hunted. Eventually the population started dying out. A petition was passed on a thin thread in hopes to spare some of those who acted more civil.

The few that were spared were branded with the dire wolf insignia, so nobody would forget what they were. And any of those who reproduced would pass on to their offspring both the brand and the reputation that it came with.

But that was ancient history. It was assumed long ago that they had went extinct. That the last of them had finally died out.

Now as I stare at one in the flesh— the flesh of my mate— that all changes.

Riot Sydney is the descendent of a dire wolf.

Aimee was right.

A different breed of werewolf.

My hand had been lingering over him, itching with the desire to run my fingers over his skin. I pull it back quickly and step away.

"Um, goodnight," I rush out, my mind so blurred that I can't even begin to think. I close the door behind me, hoping he doesn't notice my hurry as I hasten down the hall toward my own room.

This shouldn't change anything, but it does. That symbol is a large part of his past. A dark part at that. A part so potentially full of secrets that it seems toxic.

It makes me realize how little I actually know about him. My only prior knowledge of him is that he's an infamous tyrant in exile. Now I find out that it gets even more despicable?

I burrow into the blankets of "my" bed, wrapping them loosely around me. I shouldn't be tired since I've slept so much lately, but the mental exhaustion is wearing me down. I stare at the sheets blankly until my eyes start to burn. It's not until I finally blink myself out of the trance that I realize I'm pressing my sleeve against my nose and mouth. Inhaling Riot's scent as I fall asleep in a daze.

• • •

When I wake up in the middle of the night there's no scratching in the hall. No tormented sounds or jingling of the door knob. It uneases me more than when it was there.

Crawling out of bed as if I'd never been asleep, I tread lightly down the hall to Riot's door. I hesitate, my hand hovering over the knob.

There's an aching pain in my chest, telling me that he's hurting. It takes all of my effort to hold back a whimper from my wolf. And even then it's not enough. The sad, pathetic sound leaks out.

The door is yanked open, making me jolt. I manage to catch only a glimpse of a figure standing there before arms wrap around me and pull me inside.

He pushes me against the door as it clicks shut, trapping me between it and his warm body. The burning hot skin of his torso melts through my t-shirt as he presses against me.

His head dips down, nuzzling his face in the crook of my neck. He breathes in deeply, dragging his nose across my skin. Despite the heat radiating from his body, I shiver.

Past his shoulder I can see that his bed is in a mess. The sheets are twisted and sprawled everywhere, pillows strewn across the floor. His fingers dig into my wrists with a death grip.

"You haven't slept?" I barely get the words out, my breathing shallow. His head rocks back and forth on my shoulder, answering 'no.'

"Stay," he murmurs against my hair. That single word makes my heart flutter. I can't quite tell if it's a plea or a command. Either way, I nod silently.

He steps back and walks to the bed. I follow, crawling into the opposite side of the bed. My back faces him, about two feet of distance separating us.

A few minutes pass of staring at the back of my eyelids, fully awake. My fingertips worry at the material of my shirt as I try to relax.

A low growl behind me makes me stiffen. It stops with a sudden, louder note. The bed dips and the sheets rustle as Riot tosses and turns, smaller frustrated growls coming from him.

I tingle with the instinct to comfort him.

Why am I so bad at this?

Taking a deep breath, I roll over to face him. His hands are pressed against his face, his elbows sticking up in the air.

I banish that two feet between us, sidling up to him and throwing my arm across his exposed stomach. I use the side of his chest as a pillow, warm tingles shooting through my cheek.

He tenses beneath my touch. Right when I brace myself to be shoved off, a large arm drapes across my back. It pulls me closer against him.

I wait for the tension in his body to dissipate, but it never does. His muscles stay rigid, making it the equivalent of hugging a thermal stone statue. I frown against his side and let out a long sigh, the hot air only blowing back in my face.

As if sensing my aggravation, a hand comes up to brush my hair behind my shoulder. Tentatively, he touches my ear, taking the thick metal piece pierced into the cartilage between his fingertips.

"Visari," he states, playing gently with the metallic green ring.

Every wolf has a permanent ring in the top of their ear. The color differentiates pack affiliation, each color symbolizing a different pack. The rings are wide, around three millimeters thick, and made with an unbendable steel. Once it goes in your ear as a newborn, it never comes out.

I nod against his chest, mumbling a soft "yes."

He's quiet for a couple of seconds. "Go to sleep."

That's the last thing either of us say before the silence takes place for the rest of the night. About an hour in, and I feel Riot relax beside me. A small smile cracks my lips as I close my eyes.

• • •

A long, satisfying groan leaves me as I stretch my arms above my head, waking up. My eyes open to an empty bed, Riot's lingering scent the only proof that I didn't sleep alone.

Not thinking much of it, I get up and enter the bathroom. The air is hot with steam and heavy with the smell of body wash, signaling that he was here recently.

Dismissing it, I wonder back into his room to look through the dressers, once again scraping together a pair of clothes with sheer guessing of the drawers. Taking my newfound outfit back into the black marble themed bathroom, I quickly strip down.

Just as expected, the water is already hot when I turn the shower on.

I take my sweet time in there, letting the pleasant stream massage my back. Somehow, my mind drifts to Nathan.

Today is the day I would've married him against my will. The day I would've turned into a puppet at the end of his strings. But instead I'm here, in a cabin I don't know the location of, trying to teach the meaning of the mate bond to an exiled tyrant.

Oddly enough, I'm grateful for the change of fate.

After stepping out of the shower and taking a towel from the cabinet, I begin drying off. The plush fabric is soft against my skin, encouraging me to take my time. When I stand up from drying my legs, I come face to face with myself in the mirror above the pristine sink.

My blonde hair, naturally highlighted with darker streaks, lays in wet, straight strands reaching down to my naval. Realizing how exposed I am, my hands raise the towel up in front of me, covering my stomach from view. Shifting my gaze up from there, it lands on the reflection of the metallic green ring, a convenient distraction.

Visari, the word comes to mind.

My pack. Just the name comforts me with a feeling of nostalgia. Even if a good portion of my memories are painful, that's not the land's fault. It was Alpha Andre's and his egotistical son's. It makes me wonder if I'll ever step foot on that territory ever again. I have no idea where I am. Even if I could go back, would I even want to?

A series of banging through the walls catches my attention. I hold my breath on a whim, listening as it gets more frantic.

So some of my original concepts were introduced in this chapter; the ear rings and the whole dire wolf thing. It's the little things like that that make me love this world I made so much lol.

Please feel free to share your thoughts :)

Thanks for reading!

16 | I'm Still Here

It suddenly stops. A few seconds of silence pass, then it starts again. Something ramming against the bedroom door. The sharp crack of wood snapping sounds out as it gives in.

I scramble for the clothes on the counter and throw them on with record speed; an oversized white v-neck and black sweatpants hanging loosely on my hips. My frantic hands fumble with the drawstring, pulling it tight only to drop it again.

The banging is drastically louder, now at the door of the bathroom. I barely get it knotted before the only barrier between me and whatever the hell is out there falls to the floor.

A bleach blond barges in, his alert eyes scanning the room before finally landing on me.

"She's here!" He shouts over his shoulder before turning back to me.

His face is vaguely familiar and the ring in his ear matches mine. He's from my pack, although I can't remember ever speaking to him before. I can hear Aimee's humorously exasperated voice in my head, "That's because you don't speak to anyone."

When all I do is stare, he breaks the silence for me. "Nathan sent us to take you home," he says.

The look on my face must be misleading, because his tone turns soft and comforting. Like the fear-me-not way you would talk to a child on the verge of tears.

"It's okay," he says gently, as if he's wary of his words, "He won't get you again."

Then it clicks.

They're trying to save me.

They think I was kidnapped. Which technically is true, but by my mate. Does that even count?

A short haired brunette bursts through the doorless doorway, sharing the blond's highly alert energy.

"Get her and let's go. He could be back at any second," she barks before turning and leaving just as quickly as she'd came. I'm an object to them, that's clear to see. Nothing more than an objective in their rescue mission.

At her orders, the blond steps aside and gestures with his hand.

I give him a cynical once-over. The fact that they think I'd ever want to go back is appalling. During my punishments they shunned me, too; the entire pack did. Yet there's a guilt that weighs heavy on my mind.

There's someone I left behind there. The only person who ever cared about me. And in return I disappeared without telling her goodbye.

They'll show me the way back and then I can gain my bearings as to where I am. Once I explain this to Aimee, I'll have no obligation to be there any longer. But what about Riot?

What will he do when he realizes I'm gone? It's a crazy thought, irrational at best, but I might be able to make the trip and back before he returns from wherever he's gone.

Finally, after biting my lip hard enough that it begins to sting, I nod. I follow the boy through the bedroom, down the stairs, and through the living room.

I'll be back, Riot. Just trust me.

I hesitate again at the door, like an invisible force is pulling me to a stop. Something gnaws at my conscience, something that makes my wolf whine. I shake my head and push it away as I shut the door behind me, catching up with my walking compass.

"How do you know he's gone?" I ask, my eyes grazing over the edge of the forest, where the trees become denser. There are three wolves sitting in the distance, watching us and our surroundings like hawks. I can't help but to feel like that giant, rage-induced wolf is going to leap out of the shadows, just like the night of the ceremony.

"We've been watching the house for a while now. He left about ten minutes ago, off the other way. Don't worry. You're safe now," the blond reassures with a calm, level voice. He's been trained well. I know the comforting tone he's using is fake, but he manages to make it sound genuine.

"Creep," I mumble, not even loud enough to be considered a whisper.

"Huh?"

I smile. "Lead the way."

• • •

As they lead the way I try to lag behind, but not far enough that they'd notice. One of them mentioned it once, to which I excused it as being sleep deprived for the past couple of days. They seemed to believe me.

Every couple of minutes I would scratch the bark off of a tree or stand a stick up against the trunk while they weren't looking. Occasionally I would drag my feet a bit— another symptom excused for being awake for too long— turning the leaves up in an obvious manner.

The cabin had been on a flat area on the side of a gigantic mountain, concealed by the trees. Not the mountain, but the cabin. Nothing could hide something that enormous. Even after reaching flat ground, it was a long walk until I began to recognize my surroundings.

When the Visari camp comes into view, the three who remained in their wolf forms kept walking. The blond stops abruptly, turning on me. His expression is completely different, like he took his sleeve and wiped off his stage paint.

His hand grabs my throat, shoving me roughly into a tree. His face is inches from mine, my back pressing into the scratchy bark. I suck in a sharp breath through my teeth.

"You're a terrible liar," he snarls, "I told you we watched the house. That means we saw you getting all cozy with your captor." He tightens his fingers around my neck. "Stockholm syndrome only goes so far, Adrienne."

He presses me harder against the tree with his hand, but I refuse to give him the satisfaction of watching me gasp for air.

I put my palm on the arm holding me and extend my claws. With a steady pace I inject them all the more gently into the very muscle fibers.

"Someone likes sniffing everyone's business but their own," I croak out, grimacing at my burning lungs.

He leers at me, staring holes through my face. He breaks eye contact only to glance at the claws steadily digging into his flesh. As if making a split second decision, he releases me. Gravity pulls me forward, revealing that my feet had been nearly off the ground. When he steps back blood flows from the fresh holes in his arm, dripping onto the dirt.

He acts as though he done me a favor. "Nathan is waiting for you in his office. He doesn't know. I'll let you deal with that."

He pivots on his heel to walk toward the camp with a cocky sway. He turns his head, calling a warning back over his shoulder, although I'm sure it's not meant to help me in any way. "Don't expect to be welcomed with open arms."

I rub the red marks on my neck as I watch him walk away. I stare harshly at his retreating form with hopes of him catching fire, but he never does.

The path I follow through the mountainous terrain of Visari territory is familiar and well traveled. A sense of deja vu washes over me at how many times I've walked through these woods alone.

This is the only place where freedom exists. So I came here to find it. Nobody cared to follow me up the path when I went on my runs, which meant there would be nobody to turn a deaf ear on me or shout orders in my face.

Now I'm just stalling up here, looking down on the small houses nestled in the wintry hollow. The surrounding mountains shield the camp from the weather. That's the thing about the Visari valley. It's protected. Safe.

Which is why Riot Sydney's arrival shook them so much. He's not safe, and not even our beloved mountains could protect us from him.

Taking one last deep breath, I turn off the path and head for the bleak little village below.

• • •

As I passed pack members the only acknowledgement they showed me were cold stares. None of them said anything, and I didn't bother to ask why. It feels too much like the past and the old anxiety starts prancing in my chest.

That blond bitch spread rumors. That's all.

I go to Aimee's house first, with an all too familiar "screw Nathan, he can wait" mindset. She isn't home, my repetitive rapping on the door proving as much. A dusting of snow covers the deck of her front porch. No footsteps are disturbing it besides mine, meaning she hasn't been here in a while. Somehow that makes a pang of worry settle in my stomach.

The only person I came back for, and she's not even here. Disappointment fills me, knowing this was my last chance to see her. To explain myself to my best friend.

I stall for a while longer, sitting on the bench on her porch. I watch whirlwinds of snow dance in the distance, manipulated by the breeze.

Time passes and still no Aimee.

Giving up on waiting, I decide to rip the bandaid off.

I don't knock when I reach the Alpha's door. I open it slowly, peeking my head inside before my body follows.

Just as expected, Andre and Nathan have taken their house back now that Riot's done renting it. Their scents fill the area fully, restoring their claim over it. Not a single trace of the tyrant remains. I'm confident they've made sure of that.

I find Nathan at the desk in his father's office. An office that would've been his if things had gone as planned. He looks upon my entry and his eyes seem to brighten a fraction.

"Adrienne," he sounds relieved. As if realizing that himself, his eyes flicker away from mine. When they come back, his attitude is changed; more business-like.

He flips open a magazine on his desk. "Come pick out your dress."

I raise an eyebrow. "Dress?"

"The wedding is postponed until tomorrow. There's not much time to get all that ready," he gestures up and down my body with his hand, "So we're starting now."

A pang of agitation shoots through me. He really isn't letting it go, is he? A forced marriage, what more could he want from life?

"I would slit my own throat before I say a single vow to you. Find some other bitch to blackmail," I snap, my voice dripping with hatred.

I don't know what's sadder; the scumbag sitting in front of me or the fact that I mean exactly what I say.

He stands up from his desk abruptly, no doubt with an aching ego. "Oh and I suppose you'd rather go back to the bastard who dragged you off," He retorts sarcastically, as if that would make me leap into his arms over the alternative.

Something then comes over me, a sudden anger blossoming in my chest. I barely catch my growl before it can slip out through my growing canines.

"You mean Riot?"

"Riot," he laughs bitterly, "That's one word for him. That mutt is nothing but a waste of oxygen."

My fists clench at my sides. "And you're not? Oh, that's right. You replace it with all the hot air you blow. Besides that, it seems to me like that waste of oxygen kicked your ass pretty easily."

A low and provoked growl rumbles through him. It satisfies me in knowing that I've hit a nerve.

"Why are you defending him," He asks, although he's the one with the defensive tone. Even from all the way across the room I can see that prominent vein rising in his neck.

My arms cross over my chest and my weight shifts as I give him a calculating stare.

The natural light leaking in the windows has been fading and is finally gone now. Outside the sky has turned grey and angry, and there's a soft thunder rolling in the distance.

"Wouldn't you like to know," I sneer.

He takes a step out from around his desk, coming threateningly closer. "I would actually. Are you going to tell me willingly or does there have to be consequences?"

I can't stop the smirk from creeping onto my lips. Something comes over me, something I'm not fully in control of. It's like my subconscious makes the decision for me.

I'll never be free here. My pointless optimism that things would work out and go back to how they were when I was a kid is gone. I know my way out and he can't threaten me anymore.

So I mock him for the first time without so much as thinking about a punishment to come later. "What are you going to do? Sick your daddy on me? Because he solves all your problems, right? Only the best for baby Nate."

His shoulders tense at the mention of his long lost nickname. He stopped getting called Nate at the same time I stopped being included in the family: when I started taking our training more seriously than he did.

But I don't stop at the name. That's only the beginning.

"That's right. I remember. Ignoring something doesn't make it go away, Nathan. You should have learned that a long time ago because I'm still here."

He doesn't respond. The storm casted shadows of the unlit room hide whatever expression he wears. The atmosphere starts to press down on us, making me feel awkward now.

When he doesn't speak, I answer his question quietly, yet plenty loud enough for him to hear.

"He's my mate. If you really wanted to know."

-

What are your predictions for what will happen? Where's Riot and what will Nathan do now that he knows the two are mates?

Thanks for reading!

17 | Demons

"What?" His voice is strained and shaky.

I know that tone. That's the way he always talked when we were kids and he was about to have a fit. Nearly seven years later and that's the only thing that hasn't changed about him.

"He's. My. Mate," I repeat, emphasizing every word like I'm rubbing salt in an open wound. "Did you get it that time?"

He laughs, trying to cover up the twitch in his eye, but it's an empty sound. "That's tragic then. Because that doesn't change anything. You're already taken."

A roar of thunder comes again, like it's in tune with my emotions.

"It's funny how he kidnapped me yet he still treated me more humanely than you ever will again," I say sourly. I turn on my heel to leave, sick of even looking at him.

"Where are you going?" He calls angrily. His footsteps trail behind me until they catch up. Like a sixth sense, I can feel his hand reaching out for my arm.

I spin around on a dime, my eyes black as I snarl in his face.

"Try to touch me and see what fucking happens," I snap, my voice so firm that it almost breaks.

He freezes in place as he makes his decision, then takes a cautious step backward. I can hear him swallow, the sound amplified by the silence. It makes me want to lunge for his throat so it never swallows again.

"Your stuff is being moved here," he says quietly.

I raise an eyebrow at the audacity of his wording. He truly is trying to act like it didn't happen. So I decide to correct him.

"You mean being moved back?"

He grimaces, almost as if he's ashamed of something.

I shake my head and storm away. If I stay near him any longer then that thin line of control could easily break. And murder charges are the last thing I need, especially against the Alpha's spoiled son.

I storm down the hall, fuming to the point that I can't think straight. I leave Nathan's house, regretting ever going in. I simply walk without thinking, and somehow, my legs lead me to a rock face that helps to form the natural walls around our camp.

This side of the barrier, however, has an opening. An archway carved into the stone of the cliff. The stairs within lead into the underground, a massive cave made into the rock.

As I descend down a heavy feeling settles in my stomach. Everything is the same as I remember it— the glistening lake thirty foot below where I walk, the silver bars in the wall that seal off my chamber from the rest of the world. The only thing different is that there are no guards standing point to shun me.

As soon as I peer through the bars, reality washes over me like a flood. I realize that my eyes are hot and my vision is blurred. My breathing becomes shallow and shaky as I stare at the bare, short corridor. It splits at the end, the corners hiding what's further in the cell in either stone hallway.

My mouth goes dry when I see a small orange roll of paper laying on the ground in a pile of smeared ashes. I notice I'm squeezing my own hand, the knuckles of one pressed into the palm of the other.

Why did I come back? It's not like I'll miss it.

It's been a year and a half. The longest I've ever stayed out uninterrupted. Now that record is being threatened.

"Miss it?" A deep voice echoes in the cave. I turn my head, but the rest of my body is cemented in place.

My response is immediate, and somehow, composed. "No."

"Then I would watch that mouth of yours. Are we really going to have this problem again?" Alpha Andre comes to stand beside me calmly, facing the chamber just as I am. He talks in a soothing manner, "Nathan told me about your little scene."

Of course he did.

"What else did he tell you?" I ask.

"That you've found your mate," he looks at me from the side, "That he's the Exiled Alpha. Correct?"

I swallow and nod.

Andre looks back to the empty cell. "That complicates things. But you're still to be the Luna of this pack," he pauses, speaking slowly and simply, "You're going to pick Nathan over him. And if you don't..."

He nods his head wordlessly toward the cell.

I finally find it in me to move, stepping back and angling my shoulders to face him.

"I'll think about it," I lie through my teeth.

He gazes at me, a doubtful gleam in his eyes. "I'm sure you will."

I saunter past him, resisting the urge to bump his shoulder aggressively with mine. I keep my pace slow, trying to hide the fact that I'm falling apart on the inside.

Snapping at Nathan is one thing, but disrespecting the Alpha is another. I learned where that boundary lay long ago. Whether I always acknowledge it or not is up for debate.

As soon as I reach ground level, a gust of wind hits me in full force. All of the leaves rustling across and blowing across the ground makes a soft static in my ears. A streak of lighting flashes in the distance, the loud crack coming seconds later.

I push against the wind as I make my way towards the Visarian settlements, my hair whipping behind me. People rush into their houses, doors and shutters slamming to ward off the storm.

I make a beeline for my room, basically leaping up all the stairs until I reach the loft at the top. As soon as I open the door I slam it shut with a snarl.

Half of my belongings are gone. My closet is standing open, nothing in it besides empty hangers. The dresser drawers are pulled out, completely bare inside. The fairy lights are gone, as is anything else that was hanging on the wall. The room looks naked.

I go straight to my desk, praying that what I need is still there as I jerk open the top drawer. I breathe a sigh of relief when I see it.

Maybe it's all the memories of the past that push me to pick up the red box covered in bold warnings and disclaimers. Maybe it's the nostalgia of going down there again that makes me pull one of the sticks from the carton as old habits resurface.

I spark the lighter and light the cigarette, trying to numb the pain just like I did when I was at my worst.

I put it between my lips and inhale deeply, closing my eyes. When I open them again I blow out a long drag of smoke, coughing as my lungs readjust to the familiar stimulation.

My hand shakes as I hold it between my fingers.

Just like that, that same dark place is dragging me back again. The smell of the smoke makes me sick to my stomach, bringing back the view from the other side of those silver bars. I can hear the silence, minus the soft rippling of the lake and the annoyed breathing of the guards.

Out of the blue my mind snaps back to Riot.

I don't have to choose like Alpha Andre wants me to. I can't. It's impossible to choose when there's only one choice.

Three curt knocks come from the door, pulling me out of my own head.

Even through the smoke I can pick up Nathan's scent— one I've come to loathe.

I move without thought: dropping the cigarette and grinding it into the carpet with my shoe. I go over to the window and slide it up. My legs go out first, and my knuckles turn white from my grip on the sill as I brace myself for the fall.

The shock travels from my feet all the way up to my thighs. When I lose my balance and fall forward, I catch myself with my hands on the cold dirt, quickly recovering.

The package of cigarettes in my pocket seems to burn a hole right through the pants and straight into my skin. I train my mind on anything else in attempt to forget about it, observing the few blades of grass on the ground in great detail.

I stride angrily out of the village, with no intentions of looking back. I reach the top of the ridge overlooking the houses when the freezing rain finally breaks loose.

Although it's only about noon, it looks like night time as I make my way through the forest. I wipe at the water streaming down my face, trying to find the trail I'd left myself.

A bare spot on a tree catches my eye where I'd ripped a slab of bark off. I follow the rest of the markings with ease, the only challenge being keeping the pouring rain out of my eyes.

It doesn't take long for my clothes to become soaked. By the time the cabin finally comes into view— which is an eternity and countless hours later— my legs are burning from the climb and I'm dripping wet. Strands of hair are plastered across my face, not a single dry spot on me.

The cabin is as dark as the sky, looking eerily vacant. The front door lays flat from where it was broken down early in the morning. I step over it as I enter, searching along the wall for a light switch.

When I finally find one, a large chandelier hanging from the high ceiling illuminates the room. I stare in horror at the scene, my mouth falling open.

The house is wrecked. I thought the couch in the wall and broken door were bad enough, but it gets worse. So, so much worse.

The couch is now in the middle of the room, sideways and flipped upside down. The coffee table is snapped in half, the halves laying on complete opposite ends of the room. There are obvious signs of rage, like splintered pieces of wood from the claw marks on the floor or vases shattered against the walls.

Although the moose head mounted above the fire place is the same, he looks different to me. Like he's witnessed something he didn't want to.

I wonder into the kitchen to take in the damage there. The table is in the corner, the glass part of it shattered and sprawled in a million pieces over the tiles.

I don't get the chance to look at anything else, because my eyes are glued to one thing and one thing only.

In the middle of the room, a dark furred wolf is curled into a ball among the shattered glass. It's paws are covering its eyes and its tail is tucked between its legs. It lays quivering, whimpering. Tormented.

-

As expected, Nathan and his dad are still anuses. Tell me your thoughts on the chapter :)

Thanks for reading!

18 | You Had A Choice

The wolf is so preoccupied in its own misery that it doesn't even notice my presence.

My lip quivers as a desperate, grieving pain takes hold.

I scamper over the shattered glass strewn across the tile, dropping to the floor when I reach him. I throw myself over his back and shoulder like a blanket, clinging onto him as if my life depends on it. Glass shards dig into my knees, but I don't even feel them. The pressure is there, though the pain is a ghost.

"I'm so sorry," I breathe out, my face buried in his silky pelt. I'm beyond sorry. Sorry doesn't even begin to graze the surface of what I am.

His muscles ripple beneath me as he shifts, the cracking and popping of bones filling my ears. Instead of soft fur, my cheek is pressed against smooth, hot skin.

Within seconds he's turned around and sitting up, pulling me into his lap with ferocious force. He doesn't seem to care that I'm sopping wet with hair plastered against my face. His arms lock around me, pressing me flush against him. Like clockwork, my legs go on either side of his torso and my arms wrap around his neck tightly, hugging his head against my collarbone.

"I shouldn't have left you," I murmur against his shoulder. My fingers drag across his skin as they curl into fists, holding onto him for dear life.

He inhales fervently, taking in my scent.

His wolf was making his life hell because he was fighting it. I knew that, yet I still left him alone to deal with the anguish himself.

I'm an idiot. A fucking moron.

"Riot... Say something. Please," I beg. His silence has always been frustrating, but I'm not frustrated anymore. I'm terrified. Terrified of what I might have done.

He tightens his arms around me, squeezing me. Even if I wanted to, the possibility of breaking away now is fictional.

"Why?" He croaks out against the junction of my neck and shoulder. His hot breath makes goosebumps rise on my back.

"Why?" I repeat. Why what?

He pulls back, his hands moving to grip my sides as he looks at me. Something flashes in his obsidian eyes. Something I can't even begin to understand the meaning of.

"Why did you go with them?" His voice is jaded. I can't tell if he's broken inside or building a fire.

"I had to-"

"I come back and you're just gone. Strange scents were everywhere," his growl lowers to an even deadlier level, "Mixed with yours." His fingers are digging into my sides and the growth of his claws isn't exactly subtle. Nonetheless, I hold back the wince.

"You don't know how badly I wanted to track them down and rip them limb from limb," his eyes darken as he talks, as well as his tone until the point that I see canines flashing behind his lips. "Just because their scents were on yours."

Before I can even state my claim, another foreboding growl leaves his throat. "And you let them."

He suddenly lifts me off of him, sitting me carelessly on the floor beside him. He gets up in a hurry, walking out of the kitchen before I even have the chance to blink.

Amidst the shattered glass, I there for a minute, letting the sparks of his touch fade away. In that minute I feel nothing. Emptiness. Until the anger sets in.

Somehow the blame always falls back to me. This time, however, I'm not letting it.

My pride says to follow him and argue on my behalf, but my conscience says to leave him be.

Just like when I left him here, I go against my better judgement.

"You're blaming me?" I fume as I follow him into the wrecked living room.

He pivots around on a dime, his chest heaving like it's a bomb set on a timer. When he opens his mouth, that bomb explodes, "YOU WENT WITH THEM WILLINGLY!"

"I didn't have much of choice!" I fire back, thought my volume is far from the same level as his.

I catch a blur of movement in the corner of my eye. My hand flies up as reflex and the sharp smack of flesh meeting flesh follows. I don't break eye contact as I process what's just happened. His knuckles are pressed into my palm, his fist held in my palm only mere inches from my face.

"You're not defenseless, Adrienne. You had a choice." His burning gaze is enough make any wolf crumple. But if Alpha Andre couldn't break me in the seventeen years he's had at me, Riot Sydney isn't going to in one try.

"Yeah," I say, glaring right back at him, "I did have a choice. And I chose to come back." I drop his fist from my grasp, throwing it back to his side as if to make a point. My point being that his is irrelevant.

His face is like a stone precipice; an unreadable slate looking down on me. When I begin to think he's not going to respond, he finally asks, "Why did you come back?"

I shrug. "The same reason you brought me here in the first place."

We both have questions, and he's capable of answering all of them. If playing mind games is what it takes to get those answers, then so be it.

Blackened irises roam over my face, memorizing every line and every contour. Ever so slowly I can sense the distance between us growing shorter as his body gravitates closer to mine.

"And what reason is that?" The hot-blooded timbre of his voice makes me shiver.

His fingertips graze my waist tentatively, beckoning me to come closer. I notice his lips slightly part as he leans in, his eyes clouded with something I haven't quite seen before.

"You tell me."

My heartbeat is thumping inside me, pumping pulsing blood through my veins. My fingertips and hands tingle to touch him.

Due to our close proximities, his lack of apparel suddenly becomes obvious. I resist looking down, knowing exactly what I'll see there. Heat other than his breath rushes over my face.

"Go put on some pants."

And just like that, the intensity of the moment goes up in smoke.

A quiet growl leaves him as he pulls away. Not like the life threatening ones I'm used to hearing, but one of vast annoyance.

A small smirk pushes its way onto my mouth as he steps back. It may be just my imagination, but I think I see the edges of his lips turn upward as he turns away.

Once he's gone I calm myself down by taking in the state of the house for a second time. With a drawn out sigh, I flip the couch back over on its legs and put it back to where it was to begin with, which is in front of the fireplace. I find a broom and start sweeping up the various debris thrown across the ground.

I come to a spot in the floor that's splintered and morphed something awful. Small trenches are cut deep into the wood, albeit nearly prying the boards up. Beside that, a single three-clawed mark carved into the oak peaks my interest.

For some reason I can't take my eyes off of the mark. Something inside me stirs at the sight, a strangely familiar aura coming from it. Soon I'm kneeling down beside it, gently tracing over the splintered trenches.

The quiet creak of the stairs causes me to leap to my feet, heart racing. A clothed Riot comes down them— clothed from the waist down at least.

His torso remains both without a flaw nor a shirt. Without a flaw, that is, except for the three long scars running diagonally across his right pec.

Turning the other way, I go back to sweeping. It takes me about five seconds to realize what I've missed. And when I do, my blood runs cold.

The mark on his chest matches the one carved in the wood almost exactly. The one on the floor he left in the midst of his torment, but the one on his chest...

He scarred himself... but why?

"Here," his husky, nonchalant voice snaps me out of my trance. He's holding out a pair of clothes to me.

Hesitantly, I reach out and take them from him, forcing a nod of thanks. I had completely forgotten about my sopping attire, too immersed in other things to care. I wonder off down the hall and into the downstairs bathroom to change.

No matter how hard I try or how many scenarios run through my head, I can't push out that one question. Why?

I snort to myself as I close the bathroom door.

Such a hypocrite thing to ask: why?

He has to have his reasons. Yet it's so much harder to understand when looking through someone else's point of view. From the outside in rather than vice versa. I can't even fully understand when looking through my own, much less Riot's.

Forcing it out of mind, I strip down quickly and toss my waterlogged clothes into the shower. The cigarettes in my pocket I stash away in the otherwise empty medicine cabinet. My hands seem to shake as I do.

After closing the cabinet, I glance down at my bare stomach for only a brief few seconds.

Why?

Maybe the question was never meant to be answered.

I hurriedly slip on the dry t-shirt and sweats, which seems to be my only sense of fashion as of late.

I come back into the living room to find Riot rearranging the pieces of furniture that aren't completely trashed. Without a word, I reclaim the broom and resume sweeping the floor.

Time passes in an uncomfortable silence. It's been nearly an hour of quiet cleaning, and even then the house still looks like a mess.

I'm focused on picking up a broken vase, piece by piece, when I hear a loud, agitated growl.

Riot is slumped down on the couch, his hands covering his face as he looks towards the ceiling. "What the fuck are you doing to me?" He groans out. I stand up from my crouching position and slowly make my way towards him.

"I can't even be in the same room as you without feeling all fucking weird inside. I want you near me but you're so close yet so far. I have to walk around with your scent everywhere and I fucking hate it because I can't get enough of it."

By the time he's done rambling I'm standing in front of him, grinning down at my mate who once again seems so stressed out. He stares at the ceiling with glassy eyes, the whites of them tainted with little red, squiggly lines.

"Riot," I say gently, barely touching his knee, "I told you— it's okay."

He catches my wrist in his hand, steadily pulling me closer.

I sit down on the couch beside him, turning my body towards him and tucking my legs beneath me. My knee is touching the side of his thigh, and although the contact is minimal, it somehow means so much.

He still holds my wrist, showing no sign of letting go. His gaze searches my face yet again, going over every millimeter like he's sketching me in his mind.

"I hate you," he finally says.

I smile, sliding my fingers between his. "Good."

19 | Sisterly Love

The days go by in the blink of an eye, and soon a week has passed. We repaired the house to the best of our abilities, although the holes are still in the walls and the claw marks in the floors.

We still sleep in separate rooms, although there's an unspoken discomfort there. Riot's wolf has calmed down substantially, making the nights more peaceful. The days have been spent fixing the house. Now it finally looks lived in and not abandoned, nor the target of a tornado.

I've grown used to random, inconsistent acts of affection from Riot. We still aren't close physically, but he's stopped fighting it as much. On any occasion it's become normal for him to touch me in the smallest of ways. Like appearing out of the blue just to put his hand on my arm, or hovering near me while I do whatever task is at hand.

If Alpha Andre or his son are angry at my disappearance, they haven't made it known. Which has only puts me more on edge. With every noise I hear outside I expect to see the door I just put back up to come crashing down again. But it hasn't yet.

My dreams have become hell and it's always the same one. Where I'm back on Visari territory with faceless people staring at me silently. Every time it occurs, I resort to the cigarettes to calm me down. I don't tell Riot; about the dreams or the smoking. If he's ever smelled the smoke— which I've gone to great lengths to hide— he hasn't mentioned it.

I've spent so much time in the cabin that I start hating the view of it. Back home I took to the trails as much as possible just to get away. I know that's exactly what I need right now.

I step out onto the front porch and strip down. The early morning air is crisp and chilled, just the right temperature to be invigorating. I leave my clothes hanging on the inside of the door for Riot to see in case he wakes up while I'm gone.

Considering that I just got done running damage control from last time, I'm not looking for a relapse.

I step off the porch and shift, having missed the feel of being on four legs. I trot through the quiet forest, dawn just now breaking over the horizon. Cool shades of purple and blue paint the sunrise, the light not yet reaching through the trees.

The sky, like everything else here, is beautiful. When midday sets it turns to a clear, extravagant blue. Although it's no different than the one above Visari, it feels different. Untouched.

I remember a couple of days ago when I asked Riot how this land got by without being claimed by a pack. How an entire mountain had slipped by unattained by anyone.

He told me about a legend that it kept long ago, one that drove everyone away from it. Something about a bleeding sky and monsters coming out at more than just night. He kept it vague and I didn't bother to press any further.

Not a single bird chirps, being too early even for them. The silence is noticeable, making the crunching of leaves under my paws all the louder. Which is why, when I stop walking, the scratching of tree bark sticks out like a sore thumb.

Right as my ears perk up, a weight drops on my back. Once the air is knocked from my lungs an arm slips around my neck, not giving me the chance to get it back.

Irritation shoots through me in an instant and a fighting instinct takes over. I'm kicking, jumping, and shaking frantically, trying anything at all to throw whatever asshole is on me off. My attacker's legs slide down to squeeze my sides, hanging on tighter with a readjusted grip. The whole time, snarls are tearing from my throat as fast as my heart is pounding.

"Stop struggling, dammit!" A stentorian female voice barks hatefully in my ear.

I'm the one irritating her?

Instead of obeying, I slam my back against a tree, proving to be a fantastically ineffective way of breaking her hold.

Adrenaline pumps through my veins, but it's not enough to block out the pain. My deep, guttural growls turn into high-pitched canine screaming. A hot substance runs down my side, setting it on fire.

It feels like my flesh is melting on contact, like acid is burning all the way through my body. In an instant my attacker is plucked off of me, though it's barely noticed. I collapse onto the ground, convulsing violently. The stinging, burning pain racks my every nerve.

I find myself unable to swallow, resulting in saliva puddling by my open jaws. My eyes start to dry out and glaze over, unable to blink. Through unfocused vision I try to make out the blurry movement in the distance.

I sense Riot's presence. He's one of the two figures I see. A more agile one dodges every lunge and swing that he makes, flipping backwards like it's a gymnastics competition.

"Aw, I missed you, too," the same strange voice coos, "But if you care about her, you better hurry. They bleed out quick."

My breathing is so shallow that I begin to wonder if I even am. My muscles still try to spasm uncontrollably, but it's a lazy attempt.

Riot's presence is near me, but I can't see him. Everything has become a smear of faded colors.

"Baby, shift," I recognize his desperately gentle voice. The more he talks, the more distraught it becomes. "Adrienne? Adrienne, can you hear me?"

I think he's touching me, but I can't be sure. A long, dull ringing fills my ears, like I'm submerged in water. When it goes away, I hear Riot again. He sounds... defeated.

"...Force shift her."

Something thin and sharp sticks into my neck. No feeling follows.

• • •

My awareness comes in fragments from there. One minute I'm cradled against Riot's chest and the next I'm sitting on a kitchen counter, his scent clouding my senses.

I realize I'm slumped over, head laying on his shoulder. I'm like a boneless doll that he has to hold up. He's pressing something gingerly against my burning side.

A blanket is wrapped around me, Riot's hand slipped beneath it to hold pressure on the wound. I wince sharply when I move.

"Shh. You're okay," he whispers, his other hand rubbing up and down my back. The shock of hearing him sound so gentle helps to distract from the pain.

"You've really let the place go downhill," the same suave voice from earlier comments. The same voice I heard right before my flesh started melting off.

A girl strides into the kitchen, looking all around the room. Her body is slender, every movement she makes somehow seeming graceful. Her hair is such a light shade of blonde that it looks white. It's tied up in a high ponytail on her head, a few strands hanging down on either side of her face. Her nose, cheekbones, jawline, and even eyes contain a sort of sharp quality about them. Somewhat lithe and chiseled.

She's dressed in black, all the way from her spiked boots and skin tight jeans to her tank top and unzipped hoodie jacket. There are various strange items strapped around her legs and her waist, all of them giving off lethal auras.

"I told you to fucking leave," Riot growls as he pulls a wad of dark red gauze away, allowing me to wrap the blanket tighter around me.

He tosses them in a nearby trash can as he turns around to face her. He stands in front of me, as if hiding me from her.

He knows she's dangerous.

"I've spent weeks tracking you down," she says as she strolls along, observing the paintings of wintery mountains and snow covered wolves on the walls. "I'm not leaving until I get what I came for."

She cranes her head to observe another picture. When she does her hair moves to the side, exposing the back of her neck. My heart leaps into my throat at the sight of what's inked into her skin.

A dire wolf's snarling head.

She turns around suddenly, my gaze landing on the metallic yellow ring in the cartilage of her ear.

Yellow. Not one of the tribal packs. Who is this girl?

Her deep set eyes land on Riot for the first time since she entered the room. Her brown irises seem to carry a shadow over them, hiding her thoughts.

"You have a lot of prices on your head, brother. I think it's time we talked about those."

Did she say... brother?

They look nothing like each other. Completely different except for that black stigma on their necks.

"Romanov sent you," Riot states. It's not a question, but rather an assumption waiting for confirmation.

The girl rounds the corner of the island, taking her time. She acts so disinterested, so apathetic.

"I came on my own merit," she drags her elegant fingers over the earthy granite countertop, watching them intently. "I want to bring you back to Khopeski."

Riot seems to flinch a microscopic amount, tensing up on the spot. I sense danger radiating from him in waves. Just like the vibes you'd feel coming from a cornered animal.

I lay my hand on his back, hoping his wolf will be more reasonable than him.

"You could live normally, like mom and dad wanted in the first place," she pulls herself up to sit on the counter with ease, "Learn to abide by a pack instead of acting like a heathen."

"What don't you understand about exile, Senya?"

Riot leans into my touch, his attention never leaving his sister. In any other case I might feel sorry for her for being the target of his anger. But judging by the searing opening in my ribs, she's far from helpless.

"I already pulled those strings," she maintains, her tone confident, "Within Khopeskian walls your rap sheet goes blank. All of it. All you have to do is live idly like a good boy."

Riot laughs, bitterly. "What makes you think I'd ever go back to that hellhole of a prison?"

"This is your only second chance," she snaps. Her voice raises an octave, the calm and collect attitude starting to unravel. "The way you're going you'll end up headless on a burning stake in the middle of a street."

A low growl fills the room.

And it doesn't come from Riot.

"He can handle himself fine," I announce, "You should go find yourself a different babysitting job."

For the first time since jumping on my back in the middle of the woods, Senya acknowledges my existence. Her calculating gaze scrutinizes me down to the core. Riot moves even more in front of me, but due to the height boost of the counter, he can't hide me completely.

After an uncomfortable minute of being looked over passes, she jerks her chin towards me. "She your mate?"

Riot nods. Despite the circumstances, I can't help but to feel a jolt of warmth inside at witnessing him finally admit it.

"I thought so," Senya hums, pleased with herself. She slides off the island, managing to make even that look graceful.

She bends over and plucks a vial from one of the pouches strapped to her thigh.

"What if I told you," she swirls the purple contents around, "That this is the only way to stop that nasty little wound from spreading, and eventually, killing her? And that the only way to get it is by walking through the Khopeski gates."

-

20 | Humans Stink

"Riot, you don't have to do this," I assure him for the last time. "It'll probably heal on its own. In fact, I feel better already," I lie.

It's not that I'm particularly ready to die. It's more like fearing the tradeoff of actually going to this place called Khopeski. I've only ever heard of it before. A city accentuated with white and gold. They aren't tribal, like Visari or Oarca or Bastieel. They live under a different hierarchy. Different laws. Different traditions.

"You're bleeding through your shirt," he growls.

I look down and realize that he's right. There's a growing patch of bright red in the white material, arguing against me so Riot doesn't have to.

Soon he's standing in front of where I sit, picking up gauze off the bed beside me. He gingerly lifts up the hem of my shirt, and luckily for me, only at the side. As tenderly as possible he presses the bandage against the open wound.

With a suppressed wince, I take it from him and gesture him away. "I'll do it. Just finish whatever you're packing."

I hate being taken care of. Not that anyone's ever tried before, rather than Aimee. She's a motherly person, and somewhere along the way, I became her pup to protect. A pang of sadness hits me with realizing that I'll probably never see her again.

Riot hesitates a bit before obliging and going back to the dresser.

Reluctantly, I get up and shuffle into the bathroom, walking at a snail's pace. Even the smallest of movements sets my side and the surrounding areas on fire all over again. It takes so much to bare it that an inhabilitating lump forms in my throat.

Don't whine. Just shut up and tolerate it.

Riot has been on edge, to say the least. Ever since his sister showed up, he's stayed tense. And hearing me screaming out in pain wouldn't help his mentality in the slightest, nor my arguing that we shouldn't even go. My only hope is that he doesn't try fighting his wolf right now, or that would be the final match thrown into the gasoline.

I take a better bandage out of the cabinet under the sink. Standing in front of the mirror, I lift my shirt up halfway. The giant chunk taken out of my side is left raw and open, the blood oozing out and the flesh gleaming. Whatever concoction Senya dumped on me, it was crafted without mercy in mind.

I wrap the thick white material tightly around my abdomen, trying to stop the blood flow. I tie it on the opposite side of the wound and by the time I'm done it feels like I'm wearing a girdle.

When I walk back out, I can't seem to push the burning question away.

"Riot," I say.

He looks up from his packing immediately, his eyes alert. Instead of meeting mine, however, they land on the scarlet stain on my side.

"What's the deal with the Khopeski pack?" I ask, curious.

Khopeski is foreign to me. They're one of the packs who branched off from our ancestors' beliefs in origin and continued evolving their way of life right along with the humans, making them modern rather than tribal.

After hearing the question, Riot goes back to throwing clothes in the bag. It's as if he's entirely uninterested in the subject. Though he feeds me my knowledge anyway.

"My parents took us there to join when we were younger. I didn't like it so I left."

My brow furrows. "You were a rogue before?" Now that I think it about it, that lifestyle seems fitting for him.

"Born one," he mumbles.

That would explain why he didn't have a ring in his ear. Though if he was in a pack at one point, he would have been given one like Senya's. How the hell did me manage to get it off? And with his ear left unflawed?

Before I can ask, he snatches the opportunity away like a carrot on a stick.

"We should go," he zips the bag and tosses it over his shoulder, "Senya's waiting. Can you walk?"

He takes a step towards me then stops himself, uncertainty written all over his face.

I nod, a little too quickly. "I'm fine."

He turns to head out the bedroom door. "Liar."

"Heathen."

• • •

We find Senya outside leaning against a tree near the cabin. Upon seeing us, a smug smile curls onto her lips.

"Don't look overly excited, brother. It's a long trip. Save some for later," she prods as she pushes herself off the tree.

There's a devious gleam in her eye, whereas Riot on the other hand looks like he would pay to die.

He doesn't even acknowledge his sister before going straight off into the woods, me hurriedly following at his side. Senya is quick to catch up and soon takes the lead.

My eyes bounce back and forth between the two of their backsides. Looking at the only article of likeness they share: the threatening black stigma made into their necks, snarling a warning to stay away from their bearers.

"What's it like? Being a dire wolf?" I glance at the two of them.

Riot corrects me almost immediately, his bad attitude still present. "We're not dire wolves," he snaps.

"Descendants of them," Senya clarifies.

"What's the difference?"

Senya takes a deep breathe before answering.

"Dire wolves were more wolf than man. We follow our instincts, they lived by theirs. The ratio of human to animal in them is tipped severely toward the latter. Some dires were even so far feral that when they did manage to shift themselves back, they didn't know how to speak or even function in a human's body. That only happened in extreme cases of isolation though."

As she talks, Senya never once looks back. Almost like she's recalling the story to herself— and enjoying every bit of it. There's a gleam in her eye, a wistfulness on her lithe face. Something tells me she's got a lot of information, and no chances to share it.

I maul over her words and add it to what I've already heard about dire wolves. How looked down upon they were because people were terrified of them. Yet I continue prying.

"Everybody wanted them dead back in the day. What's it like now?"

She shrugs. "It means nothing. The kids in the city have twisted it. They romanticized it." She says the last statement with free flowing bitterness.

The more she talks, the angrier she sounds. "When people see my stigma they assume I'm from a play or something, walking around between scenes." She sighs. "Dire descendants are rare. I've never seen any others as long as I've lived. Nobody would believe you even if you told them ours are real."

I look over to Riot where he'd been listening quietly. He nods slightly, confirming most of what she'd said.

"That's in the cities," he finally speaks. "Out here people treat you like an artifact on display." He sends me a pointed glare from the corner of his eye.

I resist shrinking back at the silent accusation. Instead, I push further.

"If people have seen your stigma, then why haven't I heard any rumors that the Exiled Alpha is a dire wolf?"

"I hid it. After I figured out that nobody would just let it go," he sends a death glare my way. Another warning for me to stop.

With a bit of thought this time, I decide to drop it. This whole Khopeski thing has put him on edge enough. If he's going back to this place he hates so much just to save my life, then the least I can do is leave him alone.

We walk in silence for a while from there. It's maybe a mile before Senya decides to initiate a new subject. She whirls around, walking backwards without breaking pace.

"Have you heard of Bloodrest?" She asks, looking at me rather than her brooding brother.

"Bloodrest?" I arch an eyebrow.

"Bloodrest," she repeats, holding her arms up and out to her sides. She's gesturing to the forest all around us. Does she mean the same legend Riot didn't feel like telling earlier?

Before she can say anything else about it, Riot stops her.

"Did you bring us out here for a fucking history lesson or are you gonna lead the way?" He growls, irritation radiating from him in thick waves.

Senya wrinkles her nose up in a sneer before turning back around. "Maybe this is why I didn't miss you. Because you're so fucking bitchy."

She seems like the kind of person who could insult people and get away with it. But this time, her words hold depth. So much so that I find myself cringing back.

I look over to Riot to check his reaction. His eyebrows are still scrunched angrily and his mouth is a thin line. But his eyes, they don't hold anything anymore. Not anger and not quite hurt.

I move closer to him. Every part of me wants to reach out and comfort him, to let him feel my touch as a sign of encouragement. But I know he'll only push it away.

Nobody speaks from then on.

• • •

It feels like hours before we finally come to something that isn't more trees. In the distance I catch sight of buildings and people moving around everywhere. As we get closer the ground is hard and a light grey color. It reminds me of the stone of the chamber, yet it's different somehow.

Right through the middle of the clump of buildings runs two iron rails, lined with smaller bars going the opposite direction. On the rails sits an enormous mass of metal, oblong and hefty looking.

"Go board. I'll get the train tickets," Senya says before breaking away from us.

I look around at the crowd of people, none of which seem to be paying attention to us. I move subconsciously closer to Riot until I realize that my shoulder is pressed against his side.

"What's that smell?" I gag, quickly covering my mouth with my hand. My eyes start to water and my nose burns a bit. So many scents are mixed together, and strongly at that. Some are overly sweet and others like rotted garbage. Merged together, its overwhelming.

"Humans," he answers, his assessing eyes scanning over the crowd. "You've never been around them before?"

I shake my head.

His hand envelops mine, lacing our fingers together. "Just stay with me."

We push our way through the people— well, Riot does while I follow behind and beat down a rising panic attack— until we're climbing up a small deck of stairs where we enter the mass of metal. Inside there are large red booths lining the walls, padded with matching bright red cushioning.

Riot leads me to the one nearest the exit. He gently guides me in first, ushering me to take the window seat. My face heats up at the tingling of his fingertips on my back.

Why is he being so supportive? The only logical answer I can come up with is that he senses my anxiety in the new environment.

He sits down beside me, as if forming a barrier between myself and the other passengers. A sensation of safety washes over me as I get comfortable in my little space. Security feels foreign, yet I think I like it.

With knots in my stomach, I turn to look out the window as a distraction.

It doesn't take long to spot Senya's nearly white hair and slender figure, weaving through the crowd with ease. She squeezes through throngs of people so quickly and fluently that it's almost hard to keep up with her in the sea of bodies. It's like she's used to maneuvering in tight places.

Feeling eyes on me, I look over to find Riot staring at me.

"What's that face for?" He asks, the ends of his mouth starting to curl upward. At first I don't know what he's talking about, and then I realize my nose is stuck in a wrinkled position.

"Humans stink."

-

Opinions on Senya?

Also, in case anyone is wondering, Adrienne isn't reacting well to the new environment because, coming from a tribal pack, that means she's spent her life in the forest and henceforth away from the modern human world.

Thanks for reading!

21 | Don't Be Petty

Senya settles herself in the booth across from Riot and I. Her eyes are shadowed over again, a stony expression on her face. That's the second thing she shares with Riot: jaded black eyes.

She peers around at the humans taking their seats all around us, filling up the booths. With the mass variety of smells swirling through the room, it's beyond me how she looks so composed.

"You okay?" Riot asks, leaning over so that his mouth is right above my ear.

I shake my head.

My eyes won't stop watering. My nose won't stop scrunching up from trying to keep the foreign smells out. And the gaping bite out of my side is on fire once again. 'Okay' isn't the word I would use to describe it.

"Here." An arm snakes around my shoulders and pulls me against a solid torso. My face presses against the side of his chest, his subliminal scent pushing away all others.

I inhale deeply, relieved to finally breathe again.

"You're tribal, aren't you?" Senya observes, studying me. Not even Riot's embrace can shield me from her sharp eyes. She watches me like a predator watching a predator.

I want to shrink further into Riot, but I stop myself. Her gaze is unnerving. Like she can see everything trapped inside me with one hard look. Finding all of my flaws and storing them away.

I nod. "Visari."

Her brow raises such a small amount that it's almost unnoticeable. Almost. She doesn't say anything else and I wonder if it was a mistake to tell her.

A soft yet piercing beep sounds out and the door we'd entered through slides closed. The machine roars to life and lurches forward. The next time I look out the window, the trees are nothing more than a blur.

Minutes later, a young boy approaches our booths. He's wearing over a black vest over a white button down shirt, carrying a classical aura about him.

"How's your ride going today? Does anyone need anything?" He asks politely. He flashes a wide, toothy smile that has 'mandatory' written all over it.

"We're fine," Senya replies frigidly. Her tone is anything but warm and the belligerent undertone is even colder. I'm thankful that I don't actually need anything, because the chances of him returning later seem slim.

As she looks over her shoulder to see the waiter off, my eyes fall on the side of her head. More specifically, her ear. It's the one without the metallic yellow pack ring, the one that should be untouched.

It's not.

A small portion of the cartilage is missing at the top. Cut out.

It wasn't taken out by some freak accident, either. It's shaped oddly, almost like a little key.

Any other time I might resist asking such a personal thing. She took an entire chunk out of my side in mere seconds with whatever deadly liquid she poured on me, and I'm not fond of the idea of testing her patience any further. But something about Riot's presence next to me makes me feel untouchable, fueling me with reckless confidence.

"What were you notched for?" The words are out before I can think about regretting them.

Every tribal pack has their own rules, but they all share the same punishment method. Whenever a wolf commits a crime, a small piece is taken from whichever ear doesn't have the ring. The procedure is done by a shard of metal being heated over an open flame until it's hot enough to melt the cartilage. Once it is, a metal pen is used to draw and retrace the shape until eventually the piece falls out. They call it Notching.

Though Notching is only used by tribal packs. Senya comes from a modern pack; Khopeski. It's strange that she would be notched.

The side of her mouth turns upwards into an embittered smirk at my question. "Not everyone looks kindly on bounty hunters."

Bounty hunter?

That would explain the numerous things she has strapped to her body at the ready, and how impossibly graceful every one of her movements are.

"I got caught one time," she holds up a shaking index finger for emphasis, "And I'm smelling my own flesh burning."

"Wouldn't know what that feels like," I mumble sarcastically. Funny. It's almost like she forgot she intentionally barbecued half of my body.

She rolls her darkened eyes. "Don't be petty," she says as she stretches her legs out across the seat. She leans back and closes her eyes, clearly settling in for a nap. Good. Maybe I'll be able to forget her existence for a short period of time.

I look over only to realize that Riot is drifting off as well. I can tell how hard he's trying to stay awake by the way he's batting his eyelids and occasionally jerking his head back up.

My lips curl into a grin as I study him. He doesn't look so tense. Maybe it's just the need for sleep that's dulling his alertness, but I choose to perceive it in a different way. One that tells me that he trusts me enough to doze off beside me.

Then it hits me. If he falls asleep on me like this, I'm done for. The static-like pins and needles would overtake my entire body and the odds me getting him off without breaking open my wound again are nonexistent.

But I can't let him be miserable the whole ride.

"You can sleep if you want." I sit up straight, which sends his eyelids shooting open.

He shakes his head frantically, "No, no. It's fine." He glances around at the surrounding booths, as if he expects someone to be plotting our deaths this very instance.

"Riot," I laugh, "If anything happens, I'll wake you up."

Before he can object, I'm re-positioning us so that my back is leaned against the wall and my legs are criss-crossed in the seat. I pull him down so that his head is resting in my lap. He doesn't resist, which only makes my wolf all the more excited.

His hand grasps my arm, reminding me of how one little touch is all it takes to calm him down when he has an episode with his own wolf. Before I realize it, I'm smiling like an idiot and trying to beat down the building desire to hug him as tightly as a koala does its tree.

With this strong of a reaction from such a small gesture, I don't even want to imagine what he felt like after fighting it for so long. The hell he must have went through.

My fingers find his coppery brown hair, running slowly through it. A satisfied growl comes from his throat, almost like a purr.

Across the aisle I catch a man and a woman, both humans, staring. Their lips are pulled back in grimaces. I glare back at them as hard and intensely as I can. As soon as we finally make eye contact, I flash my canines in a silent snarl.

Their faces flush of color as they scramble to get up and hurry towards the front of the aisle.

That's right, go cry wolf to whoever listens. Then we'll see who ends up in the mental asylum.

"This is your idea of handling things?" Riot asks, looking up at me with a raised brow.

"It worked, didn't it?"

He snorts as he closes his eyes again.

"Savage tribal," he mumbles.

"Exiled tyrant," I retort.

• • •

Riot clings to me the entirety of his nap. Every time he would squeeze me tighter, I would squeeze his hand in return to prove that I'm still here. The simple action always seemed to satisfy him.

It's hard to believe that at one point in time the entire population was so scared of these creatures that they wanted them slaughtered. I'm sitting here with possibly the only two dire wolf descendants alive and both of them are out like lights— one even using me as a teddy bear.

But those eyes? They match perfectly with all of the stories.

I shudder at the mere memory of obsidian irises, the background of which glowing a dark, ruby red. That wave of danger they sent out... I don't want to remember it.

A man stands up at the front of the room and announces that we've reached our destination. The humans all begin to flood out, their chattering creating a low hum in the atmosphere.

"Riot." I give him a slight shake. Nothing.

"Riot," I say, louder this time. No reaction.

"Alright then."

With a grand gesture of strength, I give him a shove. He lands with a thump in the middle of the aisle, an enraged growl following soon after.

Can't say I didn't warn him.

It takes him only a nanosecond to get up. Once he's back to his full towering height, he takes a threatening step towards me and I hold my hands up in defense.

"I'm already wounded, remember? You wouldn't hit the injured, would you?" I hold my side dramatically. The wound still sears with a vengeance, but it isn't nearly as bad as the initial agony.

He picks up the only bag of belongings we'd taken from the house and throws it over his shoulder.

"You'll heal," he mumbles lowly. And suddenly, I'm regretting my method of waking up the beast.

I happen look over at Senya and it's like she can feel my eyes as soon as they land on her.

"If you touch me I'll finish killing you," she growls, sitting up. Her once high and flawless ponytail is smashed and hanging loosely, ready to fall out. A large red mark runs across her cheek like an eyesore.

Riot growls. But this time, there's nothing playful about it. It's a warning.

"Lay a finger on her and I'll do more than just kill you."

Senya stands up, maintaining equally intimidating eye contact with him. Her shoulders are squared with his, and her chin held just as high. She remains silent, but her words are clear: "I'd like to see you try."

I breathe a sigh of relief when she starts to leave, then take it back when she pauses beside him.

"I'll see you behind the walls, brother." She presses something firmly into his palm. "House 18C. Romanov will be waiting for you at the Citadel at midnight. If you don't come to him, he'll come to you. So don't be late."

With that she shoves his shoulder roughly with hers, brushing past him and down the ramp. By now Riot and I are the only ones left, everyone else having already departed. I look at him and he looks at me.

It feels like an eternity before he finally holds out his hand. "Come on."

-

Yay, I updated on time! Opinions so far? What do you think waits behind the walls of the Khopeski pack?

Thank you so much for reading! It really does mean a ton because I haven't been active lately so I really don't deserve your reads anymore so if you're still here then <333

22 | Only A Descendent

Nearly a whole day. That's how far away I am from the cabin in the woods, and even further from my home.

Home. I almost laugh at the word.

Home is a place where you can always go to seek refuge and comfort. The Visari territory is a place I can never go back to. Not as long as Andre or his narcissistic spawn hold the title of 'Alpha.'

So no, the Visari pack isn't my home anymore. So where is?

Beside me, Riot tugs on his disheveled hair for about the millionth time.

We're walking along a towering stone wall, one I have to crane my neck to see the top of. The closer we get to the large golden gates in the distance, the more anxiety I can sense rolling off of my mate. The big infamous Alpha is nervous? I never thought I'd see the day.

"You're gonna go bald," I comment. "And I'm not waxing your head when you get sunburnt so you might as well stop."

Suddenly he growls, loud and thunderous. Okay... guess somebody's not in the mood for jokes.

"I smell your blood," he grits out.

"Yeah? What else is new?" I say sarcastically.

The wound had started bleeding through the bandage again. My shirt is so oversized that it hasn't gotten into the red mess yet. Although I didn't think it was bad enough to smell yet either.

He comes to a sudden stop, grabbing my wrist and jerking me to face him. "Why didn't you tell me you were bleeding again?!"

"What would you have done? Thrown me on the ground and started open surgery?"

He growls louder, almost a roar. "Adrienne, you could fucking die! Stop treating your life like it's a joke!"

I snort. "Isn't it though?"

He makes a grab for the hem of my shirt, but I dodge his hand just in time. He follows me and tries again, this time with me smacking his hand away.

"Let me see," he warns with a deadly undertone.

"No."

He lunges at me in a slew of mumbled curses, catching me between his arms. My back is pinned against his chest, his growl rumbling lowly in my ear. As he's reaching for my shirt again, a spike of adrenaline kicks in. I smear my palm against his face, trying my damnedest to push this big bastard away and disorient him in the process.

"Get off of me!"

Something warm and slimy swipes across my hand. In an instant I jerk it back, mortified. Did he just...

"YOU SICK FREAK!" I wipe my palm frantically against the side of my leg, hoping that if I rub hard enough then the spit will just disintegrate.

He takes my moment of weakness as his opening. The side of my shirt if halfway up before I can retaliate by doubling over and bear-hugging his arm, as if strangling it would actually work.

"That must be them." Somebody whispers and both of us freeze.

"Who else would it be? Hurry up, open the gates!" A voice hisses back to the first.

Riot and I's heads snap up simultaneously. There are two guards who are glancing warily at us as they scramble to push the large golden gates apart. Senya must have told them to expect us... among other things.

With a dignified glare towards Riot— one which he returns— we start forward again on the sidewalk as if the altercation hadn't happened.

"Riot Sydney. I didn't think we'd ever see you again," the guard to the right, the one furthest from me, speaks.

"That sister of yours really knows how to get her way, doesn't she?"

Before he can even answer, the guard on the left joins in.

"Who's this?" The man looks at me curiously. "Don't tell me you've found your mate after all this time. Damn, she must have a high tolerance."

"Only for alcohol," I mumble while keeping my eyes on the ground.

I earn a hearty chuckle from the guard before Riot abruptly pulls me in front of him, away from the man. He places his hand on the small of my back, guiding me forward.

He doesn't respond to them. Not verbally at least. A tense silence falls all except for the sounds of their armor shifting as they scramble back to their posts. When I glance over my shoulder I catch sight of Riot's black irises. That's all I need to see in order to know how he shut them up.

This way he handles people, he doesn't use his words. He uses intimidation. I can't help but to wonder at that.

I remember with dread what Senya had told me.

"Some dires were so far feral that when they did shift back, they didn't know how to speak."

But Riot isn't a dire wolf. He's only a descendent of one. So that doesn't apply to him... right? She also said that that only happened due to extreme cases of isolation. Which would make sense with his exile— if he were dire wolf.

Inside the Khopeskian walls, it's as beautiful as it's rumored to be. The city is tiered, smaller stone walls built into the ground to separate each other. The houses are all made of white brick and trimmed in shining gold.

Pink rose bushes line the brick street we walk down. Lampposts stand between the bushes, just starting to light up as the sun sinks behind the distant mountain, outlining the city horizon in light.

"This place is amazing. Why'd you leave?" I look around in awe, wandering down the middle of the street.

That was a dumb question. If beauty was enough to make a person stay somewhere, I would still be among the green forests of Visari.

"It's not important," he answers from behind me. I had walked ahead of him in my excitement and he doesn't seem interested in trying to keep up.

"So? I want to know."

I absentmindedly pluck a rose from a bush, feeling the soft petals between my fingers.

"Too bad."

"You called it a prison."

"Because it is."

Ugh. Having a conversation with him is like teaching a rock to communicate: impossible. It only enforces the fears already in the back of my mind.

I slow my pace, falling into line behind him. He leads us up a winding sidewalk on a hill. Giant oak trees provide a natural roof over it.

At the top there's a single, two story house. It's architecture style matches the rest of the city: white bricks and gold accent. There's a little porch on it with rows of purple flowers leading up to the stairs.

On the wall beside the door there's a metal plate. In gold lettering, it's engraving reads 18C.

Riot pulls out a key to unlock it, opening the door to the pitch black inside. Before my wolf's night vision can even kick in, the door slams shut behind me. My legs are swept out from under me and my uninjured side is pressed against a hard torso.

Judging by the movements, he carries us up a flight of stairs. I recognize the sound of a door bumping against a wall as it's swung open. Seconds later, light floods the room, forcing me to blink a bit to adjust.

He sits me on the counter of an enormous bathroom whose color scheme isn't surprising. Yep. White and gold. Considering the magnitude of this place, there's no doubt in my mind that it's all real gold at that.

Riot is in front of me. With his large hands grasped on my knees, he separates them in order to move closer. Before I can process his intentions, he reaches for my shirt. Except this time, there isn't a guard to provide a distraction.

"Riot, don't-"

He raises the fabric just enough to expose my stomach and the bandage wrapped around it. Sure enough, it's being bled through, bright red staining the crisp white.

His movements are slow, as if he's waiting on me to stop him. His fingertips linger over the end of the bandage, brushing my skin ever so faintly and forcing a shiver through my entire body. One little pull of that bandage and my stomach is exposed.

And he just so happens to be holding it between his fingers.

Like a streak of lightning, my hand is on top of his.

"I'll take care of it. Don't worry," I say, hoping my eyes don't look as pleading as they feel. I hate the fact that my voice is quivering against my will.

He stares at me intensely. His eyes darken, even more so than when he gave the guards his silent warning to back off. His jaw tightens and I know I've messed up.

"Let. Me. See." I shrink at his tone. It's deadly. So much so that I don't dare to wonder the result of opposing it.

I let my hand fall from his, lying limply in my lap.

There's no use in covering it anymore. Sooner or later, he would have to know.

With a gentle pull, the bandage unravels. It falls to my waist, exposing my bare stomach.

His breathing grows heavy, nostrils flaring with every exhale. His chest is heaving like that of a rabid animal, one who's rising aggression could be sensed from miles away.

He raises an unsteady hand, a clawed finger gingerly running over the raised tissue before firmly pressing his palm against my belly.

"Who did this?" His voice is like frigid stone, shaking with intensity.

"Nobody d-"

"WHO. DID. THIS?"

Deafening silence follows his roaring outburst. A silence that's waiting for my answer. One I don't want to give. His irises are a deep black, the dark grey wisps, almost like flames, flowing through them.

I remember my mistake the last time I pushed him. And I remember, very vividly, the ruby red glow in the dark of the living room. I remember the fear, the panic growing within— not of him, but of what he'd do.

I don't want to see that again.

I push my shirt back down and reach up to touch his face, running my thumb over his cheek.

"Riot," my voice is barely a whisper, though as clear as I can make it, "I did it."

The anger drains from his face, falling away just like his hand from my stomach. Immediately, my skin is cold without his touch.

I look him firmly in the eye, preparing to calm whatever storm is about to break loose. "It's okay."

"It's not fucking okay," he snaps, "Those are burn marks, Adrienne!" I wince at the term burn marks, picturing the horrid scars littering my abdomen. Indentations pressed into the flesh, shiny new scar tissue discerning them from the rest.

My eyes flick up to his face to see his jaw hardening. His gaze is blurred, locked on my chest but looking through me.

No more silence. For the love of the gods, no more silence.

"It was a long time ago," I offer, as if that would smooth over whatever issue is eating at him.

These are demons I buried a long time ago. Ones that I've moved past even though they're right behind me, breathing down my neck. Just like any other problem, if you don't grant it acknowledgement or concern, then it becomes powerless.

Now here they are, laid out on the table between my mate and I, seeking attention in the most desperate of ways.

"How long?" Riot asks. Although his tone is impersonal and lethargic, I'm not fool enough to believe it. My answer is critical to whichever direction this is going next: north or south.

23 | Things Changed

"**A**drienne. Look at me."

Even if I hadn't turned my cheek to him, I wouldn't be able to see him. Unshed tears turn my vision watery and staring at the tiles on the floor has become a key objective in keeping them just that: unshed.

I shake my head. "It doesn't matter. I don't want to talk about it."

I wait for his outraged objection. For another outburst maybe, telling me how stupid I am and how only a crazy person would do what I used to. After all, only someone who's insane would harm themselves, right? That's what they all say at least.

My blurry eyes widen when strong arms wrap themselves around my shoulders. When my face meets his warm, inviting chest, the dam breaks like a piece of glass. Tears flow silently down my cheeks, soaking into his dark shirt.

Damn it! Hatred for myself bubbles up in my stomach, rising until there's a lump in my throat. I thought I was over this. I thought I'd finally beat myself at this stupid game, but that's all just proving to be a hopeful mirage.

My time in the cell is over. My time at Visari is over. So why does the aftermath still follow me?

Riot tries to pull me off of him but I cling on tighter. I shake my head and mumble a stuffy "no."

He tries again, this time with more determination. Once plucked off his chest, I sit there staring at him miserably.

I don't even want to imagine what I look like right now. A puffy face smeared with tears. Red, glassy eyes that only inspire pity.

With one swift movement he brushes my hair over my head. Taking away my last resort of concealment. I feel so exposed right now that even running naked through the streets wouldn't even compare. I'd kill to be able to shove these tears back in their ducts and put on a mask to hide what's under the surface. But that's not an option.

His expression is solemn. Unreadable. But his voice is gentle, nothing like how it was moments ago.

"Tell me why," he says, just above a whisper.

I let out a small laugh along with a shrug. "I don't know. I was locked up so it was a distraction."

He goes rigid.

I've said too much.

"Locked up?" He growls, raising an eyebrow.

I wave dismissively. I don't want his wolf back. And that subject is the perfect bait for it.

His obsidian irises never wager. They stare holes into me until I finally give a reluctant sigh. My explanation is kept short. "Every time I mouthed off or did something wrong Alpha Andre would lock me in an underground cell and order the pack to shun me when I got out."

A sharp crack sounds out as the marble countertop beside my leg breaks off into pieces and clatters to the floor under his hand. His eyes are squeezed shut, as if he's stuck in his own livid head.

I'm so tired. The old emotion of dealing with dead demons has drained me and now Riot's very much alive one is stirring again; his wolf.

I lazily lean forward and toss my arms around him, resting my chin on his shoulder. "Please don't," I beg.

The inconstant vibrations from his growling stop and he goes still within my hug. I hear him suck in a sharp breath through his nose. Other than that, he doesn't move. It's as if his muscles have turned to stone beneath his skin.

Relief floods over me when he finally returns my embrace.

How the hell did that actually work?

His deep inhale against my neck causes shivers to shoot down my spine.

"Can we just go relax?" I ask, almost whiningly. As soon as I say it I realize how childish it sounds, but I don't care. All I want right now is to lay down somewhere comfortable and just... exist.

To my pleasure, he nods silently against my shoulder and pulls away. In a quick minute he finishes re-bandaging my burning side and scoops me back up off the counter.

Downstairs it's just as dark as we'd left it. He manages to find the couch among the darkness and we both sit down heavily, as if letting ourselves break then and there.

I find myself burrowing up against Riot, inserting myself under his arm and against his torso. I close my eyes and welcome that lightless place that always waits for me there.

A much valued eternity of silence passes. Nothing fills it except for the occasional rustling of fabric and the sound of Riot's heart beating calmly in his chest. Then I hear him take in a breath and open his mouth.

"Where are your parents?"

I turn around and stare at him, confused.

"Did I...?" He trails off, his gaze trained on the front door.

I blink. "No. You didn't kill them," I stop my sentence there, resisting the urge to add "when you attacked my pack."

When it seems he's waiting on me to elaborate, a strike of panic slaps me on the head. How do I even begin? This is my small, exclusive window to share something with Riot, something personal. I can't screw it up.

"I don't know them," I blurt out, afraid of my opportunity ticking away. "Andre raised me. He found an infant left in the woods, about to drown in the rain. Turns out it was me," I smile cheekily, waiting for a reaction.

His eyes darken and his brow furrows. He's perplexed, and since he's Riot, angrily so.

"He treated you like shit, Adrienne." It sounds like an accusation. A harsh contradiction to what I said about my upbringing. It stings slightly, not the way that he said it so much as the fact that it's true: my only father now treats me like a parasite.

"It used to be different," I say, the sudden—and stupid— urge to defend Alpha Andre arising. "Nathan and I, we used to be friends. Best friends. Andre raised me almost as if I were his real daughter. I lived in their house,

I was a part of their family. But things changed." I feel the spirit drain out of me as sadness weighs me down.

I can still feel his eyes on me, but they don't feel angry anymore. He's reserved when he asks, "What changed?"

I laugh. "Everything. Andre started training us. With fighting, leadership, anything an Alpha would need. But Nathan didn't take it as seriously as I did and when that started to show it became a problem."

I clench my fists, feeling my claws lengthening at remembering the violent frustration I harbor at the both of them now.

"It was always in the back of Andre's mind that I wasn't really his," I recall bitterly, "And that bothered him. It bothered him because out of the two kids that he raised it was the one unrelated to him that showed more promise. So he had to sever ties before he started favoring me over his baby boy."

I only realize that my jaw is clenched shut when a sharp ache shoots through my tooth. A finger underneath my chin startles me as my eyes are raised to meet Riot's.

"I would favor you, too." He says it without a smile or any trace of amusement on his face. He's being sincere.

I smile and huff, "You're the only one."

He takes my hand in his, playing with my fingers and running his over my knuckles. "So where did Gage come from?"

The coincidence of the situation causes me to tilt my head. "It was written on my palm when they found me."

"What about your first name?"

I give him a pointed look and slowly say, "Adri... Andre." It only makes everything all the more painfully ironic that he named me after himself as well.

But I'm sick of this subject.

"What about you?" I poke his shirt where the scar would be. Sure enough, my finger lands on one of the raised ridges.

He grabs my wrist gently and begins massaging my palm with his thumb.

"Another time."

As he stares at me I can tell his gaze is unfocused. His attention lost somewhere in his mind. If only I could hear his thoughts. Then this would be so much easier. He wouldn't be as complicated and I wouldn't be left guessing what's going on inside his head.

"We should get ready," he says, moving to sit on the edge of the couch. I groan loudly, throwing my head back with dread. The mere concept of seeing Senya again exhausts me. As if the hard feelings between her and her brother isn't enough to turn my hair grey, then the added edginess from her threatening atmosphere is.

"You're kidding." I look at him with hope in my eyes. Hope that this is all some cruel joke.

"I'm not."

"Please don't make me," I beg. He's supposed to be merciless, but maybe I can buy mercy if the puppy dog eyes are strong enough.

He leans towards me, stabilizing himself with his hand beside my hip. His breath tickles my face when he speaks he's so close. And when he does, it's low and sinister.

"You remember when you woke me up on the train?"

Oh no...

My eyes narrow into thin slits. "You ruthless bastard."

-

Should I go back to updating Tuesdays and Fridays or only Fridays? I can do either ;)

Thanks for reading!

24 | Considered Dead

An hour later and this nightmare has made itself a reality.

A silky, knee length dress hugs my body, making my discomfort levels skyrocket. The color of it is a light emerald, making the green of my ear ring stand out.

I stand on the doorstep of some looming, castle-like building on the top tier of the city. Beside me, Riot bangs the metal knocked on the door. He's also stuffed himself into formal clothes, and good lord if that suit wasn't made for him.

It looks absolutely ravishing, but it doesn't seem like the Riot I know. I keep having to take second looks at him just to make sure. Something about a suit and tie just contradicts his roguish appearance.

A servant appears at the door and leads us down a dark, stony hallway. I stick close to Riot, unsure of what to expect.

The dependence I've had of him as of late bothers me. But the fact that he hasn't been pushing me away makes it all worth it.

We come to a grand dining hall, the majority of the room nothing but open space. In the middle there's a table long enough to seat an army. At the end of it sits a smug looking man with Senya seated at the nearest side.

Romanov. That's the name that Riot and Senya had kept mentioning before. This must be the man who it belongs to.

"Ah, Riot," he greets, dragging out his name. "I'm so glad you could make it. I see you found the clothes we left for you."

Riot remains unfazed as he walks over and takes the seat opposite of Senya. With one arm he pulls out the chair beside him, a gesture for me to sit there.

"What do you want?" He asks Romanov bluntly. It isn't the nicest of tones, but at least he's keeping his composure.

Romanov smiles, as if amused. His gelled back hair blends into the shadows of the distant wall.

He slumps down, sitting as comfortably— and as informally— as possible.

"No need to rush. We have all night." He raises his hand and motions for a servant standing nearby.

In a flash, silverware and plates full of food are placed in front of us. Fancy wine glasses are also given, filled generously with their namesake.

Riot stares at the food skeptically before grudgingly picking up a fork. I, on the other hand, don't hesitate. The trip to get here was long and without luxury. At this point I'll eat anything I can get my claws on.

We all start eating, the soft clanging of metal against porcelain filling the large stony and castle-like room. It's a few minutes into the meal before somebody finally speaks

"Let's talk about all the bounties I've been receiving lately," Romanov lowers his voice a bit, "A couple dozen short of ten thousand, to be exact."

I nearly choke on my bite of potatoes.

After the initial shock of the number passes, I clench my teeth. Anger bubbles in my chest as I hold back a growl. I always knew that people feared and despised the Exiled Alpha, but I've never witnessed the full extent of the fact. I bristle at the thought of someone wishing for my mate's death. Too cowardly to try to kill him themselves at that.

Out of the corner of my eye, I see Senya freeze at the same time I do. She glares daggers in Romanov's direction. Daggers so sharp shoot from her black irises that I find it hard to believe he doesn't react to her glare burning into his face.

There's something between the two. Something hushed. But what?

"It's not that I want you dead, particularly, but this city doesn't pay for itself. And your blood is worth a pretty penny right about now."

Riot puts his fork down, as if he'd suddenly lost his appetite. He nudges his plate away before shifting a bit in his chair. I can tell that he's on high alert now. As would be expected after someone implies their intent to kill you.

"I didn't poison the food," Romanov scoffs. "That would reflect badly on the chefs. If I kill you it will be with a blade against your throat. I brought you here for an offer."

The charisma he spoke so fluently with vanishes into thin air. He leans across the table and towards Riot, venom dripping off his tongue.

Maybe this is where Senya gets her poison; from keeping company like this.

"If you stay in Khopeski then we won't have a problem. It's mostly the outsiders who want you dead. The tribals and that pack you took over, Balaige. As long as no lowlife outside of these walls sees your face, then you're as good as considered dead. I keep the money, and you keep your life."

Riot lets out an agitated growl, likely one he'd been holding in. Under the table, I reach over and place my hand on his knee. His shoulders seem to relax a slight bit.

"Give her the antidote," he says.

"You haven't agreed to the deal-"

A snarl rips from his lips, "NOW."

Romanov leers at him for a few seconds before nodding towards Senya.

In one fluid motion she stands up, then reaches down and pulls a vial from her leg. Wordlessly, she pours a blue liquid into my glass. The wine darkens, almost so that it's black. It reminds me eerily of the Sydneys' eyes.

Romanov's brow furrows, a bit of a testy tone coming with it. "I thought the antidote was purple?"

I go to pick up the glass, but Riot gets to it first. He brings it up to his nose, sniffing the contents with deathly concentration.

Once satisfied, he passes it back to me. It tastes overly sweet, as if someone had just dumped sugar in it.

"It is. The antidote was already in there. That was a placebo," she says, sitting back down. I study the glass inquisitively, wondering what the purpose of putting a placebo in could possibly be.

Unless the difference in colors wasn't suppose to be noticed.

Romanov's eyes burn angrily into Senya's as he leans towards her. He keeps his words low, like they're only meant for her to hear.

However, not much goes unheard to wolfish ears.

"I told you to wait."

"Do I look like one of your puppets?" She hisses in return.

As soon as the last drop of the remedied wine is gone, Riot shoots up from his chair.

"We're leaving."

Unable to imagine a reason why not to, I don't waste time in getting up. When I turn to look, my mate is nowhere in sight. I swallow nervously before looking back to the table.

"Uh.. Thanks for dinner," I force a smile. God, this awkward. He really had to abandon me, didn't he? First he drags me here, now he leaves me here. I knew I would regret pushing a sleeping wolf into the aisle eventually.

With a mounting sense of danger, I tuck my metaphorical tail and head for the corridor we entered from. My pace is kept just below a jog, an attempt not to make my eagerness to leave quite as obvious.

Fingers dig into my shoulder, spinning me around to come face to face with a scowling Romanov. His blue eyes are as cold as ice, yet they're just as toxic as a searing acid.

"Make sure your tyrant doesn't try for the crown," he growls lowly.

The crown. That's one of the differences in the hierarchy. Instead of an Alpha, the Khopeski pack has a king.

I narrow my eyes, challenging him. If he wants to threaten me, he'll have to try harder.

My chin raises. "Or what?"

"Or we'll have problems."

I stand up straighter at the dare, excitement buzzing inside me. "Maybe you will, but I won't."

He achieves half a step forward before Riot appears in the blink of an eye, grabbing him by his neck and yanking him away. His feet come off the ground right before he's slammed against the wall with a thud.

The smell of blood hits me. Blood that carries Romanov's scent. Over Riot's shoulder I catch sight of his claws dragging across the bottom of the other man's jaw.

Senya rushes past me and separates them with alarming ferocity. She shoulders her brother back with an agitated snarl.

The room falls deathly silent, all except for the faint heaves of Romanov and Riot catching their breath. With the elegance of a viper, Senya comes nose to nose with her sibling.

Her tone is low and scalding with warning as she does. "These people took us in when nobody else would and you weren't grateful. You weren't grateful then and you're not grateful now. They're giving you another chance— refuge after all the shit you've done— and you're still blowing it right back in their goddamn faces."

The absolute raw anger in her voice is terrifying. It's so powerful in the air that all of us take an involuntary step back from her. All except for Riot. He remains facing her, their tense and readied shoulders only inches apart.

"They killed our parents!" Riot emphasizes every word of the phrase, "If you weren't so far up his ass you would realize that!"

Both shock and adrenaline flood my system. My muscles tense, waiting for the last thread between the two titans to snap before the fight can break loose.

Senya leans back, shoulders relaxed, as if suddenly surfeited with arguing. "They didn't kill our parents," she says, a fire still burning in her.

"A belligerent rogue did," Romanov adds through spite, located a few yards behind her.

With bared canines resting behind his lips, Riot takes a step toward Romanov, staring at him with those tantalizing black eyes. When Senya blocks his path again like an immovable barrier, he ceases to acknowledge her.

Instead he turns and storms straight in my direction. His hands hold tightly onto my shoulders as he spins me around and pushes me toward the exit.

Halfway down the dark corridor, Senya's voice echoes from behind us.

"Don't show your weak spot, brother. I've already exploited it once. Don't give everyone else the same temptation." Her words give me the same chills as if a snake were hissing in my ear.

Riot gives a short, bitter laugh and without stopping calls back, "Says the dog defending her master."

25 | Buried History

"Riot! Hey, slow down, dammit! RIOT!"

My yelling does nothing to slow his pace. He's on a mission and no force can stop him. He pulls me out of the building and onto the front steps where I finally yank his arm hard enough to get the hint across.

"Are you good?" I ask, raising an eyebrow.

Riot stands at the edge of the stone stairs, both of his hands in his hair. With the suit jacket straining against his taut shoulders, it reminds just how out of place he really is.

It's midnight by now. Down below, the street lamps create golden spheres in the dark. The city seems empty all besides a lit up window here and there.

"No. I'm not." He says, dropping his hands to his sides hopelessly.

I take a tentative step forward.

"Riot, I-"

"How do you do this," He asks, looking out over the city.

"Do what?"

"Have this affect on me," he turns around, "Everything you do it makes me feel something. It's controlling." He spits the last word with spite, like the very thought of it on his tongue disgusts him.

Through the night I can still make out his features. The high cheekbones and the tiny scar cutting through his eyebrow. The roguish bit of stubble that covers his razor sharp jaw. The copper color of his eyes— meaning that for once his wolf isn't clawing at the surface.

"Maybe I'm just controlling," I say softly, taking another step, "Or maybe you're just easily controlled." I almost laugh at the irony of that statement.

Everything about him screams defeat. From his disheveled hair to his slumping shoulders and desperate looking face.

"Can I...?" He trails off, his voice strained. He doesn't want to ask, and when he does he acts as though he's ashamed for it.

"Of course." I hold out my hand, lacing it with his. He pulls me closer.

I lay my head on his collarbone and wrap my arms around him. He returns the hug, pressing our bodies flush against each other.

That's how he's been coping for the past week or so. By touch. Every time his wolf starts to flare up he has to come and touch me in the smallest of ways. That's all it takes to satisfy the only part of himself that he can't control.

It almost makes sense. For once in history, Riot Sydney almost makes sense. Being controlled is what he hates the most. It's what he loathes. And because of this, he can't even control himself.

I don't mind it though. Besides the fact, I'm happy to feel the sparks between us, too.

"When someone else so much as looks at you, it bothers me. When I saw him near you... touching you..." he growls. My heart pounds so rapidly in my chest that I think it might break a rib.

Riot is finally accepting what he feels. Finally acknowledging it. But why now? After fighting it for so long.

"Hey." I pull back, raising my hand to caress his cheek with my thumb. "I had it under control." I can't help but to grin at the line.

"I don't think you did," he says huskily. I notice his eyes fixed on my lips, their color darkening. His head starts to lower down, creeping closer to mine. I find my chin raising on its own.

My skin comes alive like it's been set on fire as soon as his lips touch mine. On instinct I arch my back, trying longingly to get closer to him. My stomach flips as though it's taken up acrobatics. His fingers curl into my sides, holding me tighter. A deep, animalistic growl rumbles in his chest, convincing me that if somebody ever tried, they would never pull me away from him. It makes me feel cherished.

My eyelids close, blossoms of warmth shooting through my body as we melt together. It seems like it lasts forever and I would give anything for that to be true. Standing in this tyrant's presence, a wolf the world claims is so vile because of his crimes, I feel untouchable. It's a high that if I were to ever come down from, would hurt like hell.

When my lungs start to burn for air— and something tells me his does too— we pull apart. We pant in unison, a smile spreading across my face.

I just kissed my mate.

After all this time, after so long of fantasizing about what could be... I finally feel close to him. Not physically close, that was never the problem. But emotionally, he's been sealed in ice.

As with every good thing, the doubts start to creep in.

What if this was just him losing control to his wolf again? What if that wasn't his actions, but rather what he couldn't consent to?

My smile drops like a ton of bricks on the pavement, chipping the stone and cracking the concrete. "Do you... Do you regret it?" I hate that I sound so pathetic. So desperate to know what he's thinking. No matter how much I may despise that, I can't deny that it's true. I need his reassurance.

In one swift movement he leans back in. And before I can blink, he's throwing my system into overdrive for a second time. This kiss is shorter. When he pulls back, his lips move towards my ear.

The slight stubble on his jaw— just enough to finish off his sexy, roguish appearance— rubs against my cheek.

"No." His voice is husky and deep in my ear. The single word makes me melt on the spot. I shiver uncontrollably, trying in vain to get myself together. My legs feel like twigs ready to snap under my weight. He's my mate, yet I'm so nervous that I'm getting sick to my stomach.

"I don't believe you. Try again." I can't get through without cracking smiling like an idiot. A feeling is bubbling inside me, like I want to burst into joyous laughter for no reason at all.

I feel so fuzzy and happy on the inside. Everything is warm and mushy and... Maybe this is why Riot freaked out so many times before.

He smirks, showing his teeth. For once, they're not razor sharps canines, but actual teeth.

He pulls me back against his chest, making my heart beat in overdrive. I lay my head against him and gaze out over the city dotted with golden lights.

His fingers run through my hair, combing it out to its full length then letting it fall gently against my back. He keeps repeating that action, each time as soothing as the last. Something between a sigh and a soft moan escapes my lips.

"Why do you hate this place so much?" I ask, watching a group of fireflies dance at the top of the distant stone wall.

"It's a long story, Adrienne."

A special feeling butterflies in my stomach when he says my name. Like I finally matter. I've heard my name said in so many different contexts; ranging from rage and irritation all the way to raw disappointment. But never in the way that it just came from his lips. And coming from him especially, the warmth sparking in my veins only doubles.

I quirk an eyebrow and look up him, my chin still resting on his chest. "I have time."

I smile up at him. He truly is the embodiment of all things visually pleasing. It's appalling to me how he's infamous for his acts of bestial tyranny rather than famous for his god-like appearance.

He opens his mouth to make a retort, and gets only halfway through his eye-roll when the slam of a heavy door behind us makes us break apart and turn around.

Senya is standing there, her nearly white hair and light complexion almost glowing in the moonlight. Her black clothes and the shadows of the Citadel's overhang only romanticize the contrast.

There's something about her and Riot that's strangely noticeable, although you only would if you knew what they were. There's something about their appearance which makes it hard to believe that more people don't realize they're a different breed of werewolf. Something scarily mythical. Something that makes you want to run the other way.

The anger and intensity of what happened inside seems to already be forgotten by her. She's once again laid-back, indifferent.

"Make your decision wisely, brother," she says as she strides slowly out of the shadow of the overhang, "Because as soon as you walk out those gates he'll start sending the hunters after you."

If Riot's annoyed by her advice, he keeps it silent. Instead he changes the subject. "Tell her," he says.

Tell me? Tell me what?

Senya nods and her shrewd eyes land on me.

"Do you know who you are?" She tilts her head at me as she asks.

My face contorts with confusion. "What?"

"You're Visarian. A real Visarian."

"What are you talking about?"

She growls lightly in frustration before continuing. "The pack you came from isn't Visarian. They just took their pack a few decades ago and kept the name."

My mind reels as the information refuses to sink in. So I come to the only conclusion I can manage.

"You knew my parents?"

She shakes her head. "No. But I have connections and I know that after the switch in bloodlines, dead babies started showing up with names written on their hands in marker."

"The Visarians were driven from their home and dying," she says as she crosses her arms, each hand holding the opposite elbow, "Some left their offspring on the doorsteps of packs in hopes that they would be given a better life, though most were found too late."

A sickening feeling squeezes my stomach. I could've been one of those babies, nothing more than a corpse of lost hope. And I nearly was, if Alpha Andre hadn't come along when he did. As negligent as he's been these past years, it's undeniable that he saved my life.

"Now," Senya says, uncrossing her arms and standing up straight, "Do with that what you will, but I would keep your mouth shut about it. It's buried history."

With that she turns and slips back through the door of the Citadel. It shuts with a soft click and the shadows in front of it settle. It's as if she'd never been here at all.

• • •

My feet are light as a feather as I bounce back to the house beside Riot. My high still hasn't come down. Not since the kiss, and not since learning my roots. It's enough to convince me to forget about everything else and just live in this simple moment.

We stroll up the hill beneath the oaks, not even a cricket's chirp daring to threaten the peace.

So I take that job into my own hands.

"Hey, Riot."

"Hm?"

I tug him to a stop at the top of the steps. The look I'm met with is smoldering, his scarred eyebrow raised in question. Waiting for me to speak.

"You had Senya tell me that, didn't you?" I grin up at him. It's just so satisfyingly amusing to watch the big bad Exiled Alpha squirm.

He fights with the sheepish smirk that's trying to overtake his lips. When he starts to lose, he looks away in the other direction. But not before I catch a glimpse of the smile reaching his eyes.

He opens the door and we enter.

"I'm gonna take a shower," he mumbles, stepping away to unlock the door. As he goes past, his fingers brush mine in a way that can be nothing but intentional. I squeeze my fist while watching him go, craving more of the sparks. My only wish is that he isn't making a relapse with his wolf.

Once he's up the stairs I growl at myself in disapproval. After giving him enough time to get situated by prancing around the living room, I head up the stairs to the bedroom. I ignore the hum of the shower as I tiptoe past.

The only bag we'd brought with us lays open on the bed. I rummage through it, wasting no time in stripping out of this godforsaken dress and changing into more comfortable attire. Then, in an inside zipper, I take what I had hid there before we left the cabin.

I make my way back downstairs and out onto the porch. In the same minute, a cigarette is between my fingers, embers glowing at the end. I take a deep puff and release the smoke into the air.

"You're letting her smoke?"

"Yeah. So?"

Their whispered voices still echo in the cavern.

"Isn't that, like... bad?"

"It keeps her quiet."

Bastards.

They were suppose to act like they didn't hear me. But I could sure as hell hear them just fine.

I thought I was past this. Yet here it is, still on my mind. Still between my lips.

"Adrienne?"

26 | Understand Me

My blood freezes in my veins at the sound of his voice. I wasn't trying to hide, per se. So what did I really expect? I feel sick with guilt, like I've done something terribly wrong.

I turn around, not bothering to hide the cigarette between my fingers. Riot is standing in the doorway of the house, his signature unreadable expression staring back at me.

Slowly, he approaches. His eyes are dead as a reaper's as he steps forward. I reciprocate with a step back. Another step forward, another step back. That's how it goes until my waist bumps into the wooden railing around the porch.

"Alright, fine. Yeah. I'm a smoker. So what?" I challenge, bracing myself for the worst. Maybe it's the suspense of the dead look on his face that gets to me, or maybe it's the guilt I already feel towards myself.

"Go ahead, tell me how stupid I am. Tell me how my lungs are blackening and how kissing me is the equivalent of licking an ashtray. Speaking of which, if you get lung cancer don't bother suing me. I'll reimburse you myself." I rant without stopping until I'm out of breath with my heart thumping in my throat. If I get all the jabs in at myself first, then he won't get the satisfaction.

While I was raving Riot was moving closer. Now his chest is inches from mine and for once the lack of distance is suffocating. As if in slow motion, he raises the hem of my shirt, exposing my stomach as if his unspoken point were written there. I don't make a move to stop him.

There they are: the various patches and streaks of raised, shiny scar tissue.

"Are you serious?" He asks, disbelief in his tone.

In the blink of an eye he grabs the cigarette from my hand and launches it across the yard. A growl thunders in his throat, aggressive enough to make a grisly bear run.

"ARE YOU FUCKING SERIOUS?!" He snarls in my face and I jerk my head away. I flinch at his volume, trapped between his body and the railing.

He snatches up pack of cigarettes peeking out of my jeans pocket. Within seconds the cardboard box is shredded in his hands and emptied on the ground.

"Hey! What the hell, you asshole!" I exclaim, although I would be more heard screaming into the void.

He stomps his foot down on the white rolls of paper, grinding them with a vengeance into the boards with his heel. With a burst of panic, I shove him away frantically. Then I crouch down, trying in vain to save the nicotine he's wasted.

But it's too late. Every single one: ruined.

Anger burns in my veins and heat rises to my face with the fury of a thousand suns. I inhale deeply, prepared to curse him out until the devil himself is taken aback. But he makes the first move, yanking me roughly to my feet.

He speaks in a deadly, strained tone. "Never touch a cigarette ever again. Do you understand me?"

When I don't answer, he repeats it even more slowly. "Do. You. Understand. Me."

I move my gaze from his chest up to his eyes. When they meet, I put as many metaphorical daggers into my stare as I can possibly muster.

"No," I snap, raising my chin defiantly, "If I want a cigarette then I'll get one. Do you understand me?"

But I'm not done there. I keep going.

"You think you're so perfect? We both have demons, Riot," I jab my finger into his scarred pec. "I know that came from your claw. So step off your goddamn high horse."

Blackened irises stare straight at me as he reaches down and pulls his shirt up, exposing the ridged claw mark. It takes an intense amount of self control not to look down and let my eyes roam over his torso.

"This is what got me my freedom," he says darkly, drilling his shirt back down. "Not wallowing in self pity."

It takes me a minute to process his words. When I do, my jaw begins to quiver. I try to decide my reaction, anything between livid and heartbroken.

Somehow, I remain calm, though only on the outside. On the inside a storm is begging to break loose.

Self pity. Why did I think he would understand? I'm a fucking idiot for ever expecting him to. I should've kept my problems hidden like I always do. It's simpler that way. So, so much more simpler.

I lower my voice and look him dead in the eye. "If you don't want ripped off then maybe you should inspect the product before buying damaged goods."

I scoff bitterly and shake my head, "Now get the fuck out of my face." Venom drips off my tongue. I want away from this bastard. As far away as the earth's boundaries will let me.

I shove past him, moving him out of the way with a sharp elbow to the ribs. I only get a steps away when a hand curls tightly around my bicep and pulls me against a rock solid chest.

"Don't touch me!" I start to struggle but his arms clamp down around me like chains.

"Listen," he hisses lowly in my ear.

His fingers dig into me, followed by his subtle sniffing of the air.

A drop of water drips down from his wet hair and onto my cheek. It slides down my neck and absorbs into my shirt. He smells intoxicating, his natural scent mixed with the fresh smell of body wash and water. I swallow the lump in my throat. I should be comfortable around my mate, yet my heart is spazzing out in my chest as he holds me.

I blink and try to focus. There's something dangerous here. That's what my animal instincts are telling me. A shiver runs down my spine with alertness. So I perk my ears, picking through the silence.

There's a rustle of leaves out by the patch of trees beyond the side yard. Riot's hold tightens impossibly further. My eyes feel ready to pop out of my head, whether it be the intensity I'm searching the dark tree line with or the arms squeezing me with enough force to strangle an ox.

I hate myself when I realize I'm holding onto him just as tight, squeezing his arm back like he's the life raft in a raging storm. As if using him as a buoy will really make the bad things go away. I wish.

I expect to hear Riot growl in response to whatever's out there, but he stays silent. He starts sniffing the air subtly, so I follow suit. Sure enough, there it is: the scent of a person, a werewolf, watching us from the shadows.

In seconds, the calm night is shattered. A snarl rips from Riot's throat as he bolts towards the presence, leaping over the porch railing like a rabid dog. I'm left feeling more vulnerable than ever without the fleshy armor he provided.

Stupid mate bond.

Without a second thought, I take off after him, vaulting over the railing with a manner of grace that surprises even me. I chase after Riot, who, in turn, is chasing after someone else. Why am I following? I have no idea.

Eventually Riot stops and I nearly slam into his back. His chest is heaving, each exhale coming out as a breathy growl.

"Romanov," he snarls, looking around the woods frantically. Patches of moonlight shine through the leaves. Other than that, everything is bathed in shadow.

I tilt my head, confused. "But that didn't smell like Romanov?"

"He sent one of his hunters," he says, nostrils flaring as he tries to pick up the trail.

That simple statement makes it all click. Romanov was hesitant with the conditions of the deal he agreed to. He was suspicious enough to bother with threatening me if Riot stepped out of line, and with the attitude he portrayed, he wasn't very confident that he wouldn't.

"He was making sure you didn't leave," I state.

His hand flexes at his side, claws curling out of sight into his balled fist. In the snap of a finger Riot is on all fours, dark fur shining in the dim moonlight. His massive paws scratch fitfully in the dirt, flinging dead leaves and unearthing damp soil. His snout moves erratically across every inch of the ground, over every tree trunk and every leaf.

I do nothing but stand there and watch, like I'm observing an animal in the wild.

Is this part of the reason he left this place before? Judging by way he's acting, the way this went straight to his nerves, I don't think this is the first time this has happened.

I open my mouth to comfort him. I even raise my hand to put on his canine shoulder, but I lower it just as quick, remembering where we stand.

If I'm so busy wallowing in my own pity, then it looks like I don't have any to spare for him.

Silently I turn and lumber slowly in the direction of the house. Fall leaves crunch loudly under my feet to announce my leave for me.

Riot is too busy with his manhunt to try and stop me. Usually my wolf would be driven mad over that and convince me that he hates me after all. But now? I'm grateful for it.

-

27 | A Safe Place

As soon as I reached house 18C I stomped straight upstairs and plopped down on the bed like a sack of wet sand. With my face buried in the pillow and the covers hugged tightly to my body, I forced sleep overtake me.

But it was restless.

I tossed and turned, huffed and puffed until the room felt hot and sticky. Like the teasing mistress it is, a good night's sleep has been avoiding me for nearly three hours.

Riot still isn't back. There hasn't been the slightest sound downstairs to indicate his arrival. Not a jingle of the door handle. Not the squeak of a door's hinges. Not even so much as a single bump in the night fabricated by my imagination. It's simply silence. And it's driving me insane. More than it ever did down in that godforsaken cave.

Eventually, when the clock strikes 3:00, I get up and throw the covers off in a tormented fit. I storm downstairs, my bare feet pattering against the wood. My hair is all over the place, frizzy and tangled. My clothes are worn and wrinkled, lounge pants rolled up to my knees. I look like an unholy nightmare, but I don't care.

As much as I hate to admit it, Riot is the reason I can't sleep. That pain in my ass made his way up to my head. And he doesn't seem to be leaving anytime soon.

He could've been ambushed by a party of bounty hunters, led straight into their trap by the spy. Or he could've went to find Romanov and settle whatever hard feelings is between them once and for all. Worse yet, he's lost control of his wolf and now he's rampaging around the city, spilling blood and killing innocents— no. Stop thinking that way.

He's fine. Everything is fine. He's probably not fine, but for the sake of my sanity, he's going to be fine.

In desperate need of fresh air, I open the front door. Then stop dead in tracks.

Night air blows against my skin, but I can't enjoy it. My jaw drops and my skin prickles.

A figure is standing there. His clothes are darkened and wet in sporadic splotches. His face looks like he's had red paint splattered all over him. Except I know that it's not paint.

The same breeze that's so refreshing carries the thick scent of blood to my nose. It's overwhelming, taking the best of my efforts not to gag.

"Riot?" My voice is frayed. I want so badly to rush over to him, but I make myself stand solid, fighting my instincts.

He looks up, a fat drop of crimson liquid running down the side of his cheek.

The look on my face must be of horror.

"It's not mine," is all he says.

"The bounty hunter?" I ask. He nods.

I try to relax, but it's impossible not to remain on edge. Cautiously, I step through the threshold of the door. I notice his fingers twitching, claws out. Adrenaline is coursing through his veins like electricity in a circuit.

"Did you see anyone else?" His voice is distracted as his eyes shift all around, checking the shadows twice. He's paranoid.

I shake my head, mumbling "No." I would've killed for someone to have turned up. Any sound to break the maddening quiet I endured, I would have been grateful for.

He doesn't say anything else and neither do I. An uncomfortable silence falls over us, which is exactly what it takes for me to realize how inconsiderate I may be coming across as.

"Uh wait here. I'll be back." I fumble as I turn and head back into the house, leaving the door wide open.

I pad quickly up the stairs and into the bedroom. The bed looks like a hurricane just passed over it, the covers laying as violently sprawled as I had left them. I go to the duffle bag in the corner of the room, digging through it on a mission.

Once I pull out a spare set of clothes, I head into the bathroom and snatch a dark blue towel out of the cabinet. At the sink I soak it in water, wring it out, and leave it wet. I gather up all the items and rush back downstairs.

Outside on the porch Riot is sitting in a chair at the edge, glaring out into the nearby woods.

"Here." I hold out the towel for him to take.

A small annoying voice in the back of mind nags at me, What are you doing? You're suppose to wash his face for him. What kind of mate are you?

I can't help but to roll my eyes. Of course that's what Agatha would say.

"YOUNG LADY, GET BACK IN HERE! You can't just leave everything unattended!!!" Her old voice would shriek as she yelled at me. It always reminded me of a dying crow.

I looked to Alpha Andre for permission. He nodded at me and motioned me off. Obediently, I ran back to the house, my little feet pounding against the dry ground. I heard Nathan's fading 'oomph' as I went, telling me he failed to dodge once again.

I barely got into the door before my ear was being pulled off by crooked, wrinkly fingers.

"OWWW!"

"Hurts, doesn't it? Maybe next time you'll learn not to run off. What business do you have out there scrapping like a dog? None, that's what."

She dragged me into the kitchen, the smell of burnt bread made me crinkle my nose. The sight of brown crust against the oven window made her shout even more when she saw it.

"What in Goddess's name did you do?!" She releases me and shuffles over to the stove. With mitted hands she threw the door open. Her jaw dropped.

The entire space of the oven, filled with a giant, bloated cloud of blackened bread.

"How much yeast did you put in?" She glared at me accusingly, her mouth bobbing open and closed like a fish.

Yeast... Which part was that again? I knew if I asked, it would only lead to another endless lecture.

"Enough?" I shrugged.

"Too much." She grumbled and began digging the charcoaled loaf out of the oven. If you could even call it a loaf anymore.

While she was preoccupied, I snuck my way back towards the door.

"Nagatha," I mumbled, so fed up with being treated like her doll.

"Excuse me?" She raised her voice behind me.

I slammed the door shut to avoid answering. And from there, I ran straight back to the training grounds.

Riot's fingers graze mine when he takes the towel. The sparks make me jolt a little, taken off guard.

As he wipes the cloth across his cheek I lean against the railing in front of him. He rubs the blood from his skin, darkening the towel with what will probably stain later.

It feels weird just standing here watching him. Somehow the silence doesn't bother me as much this time.

"I'm sorry I smoked," I finally say, embarrassed to be apologizing.

He looks up, a few dots of blood still sprinkled across the bridge of his nose. Suddenly he doesn't look as angry anymore.

"I didn't yell at you because of the smoking."

I blink. It takes a few seconds for me to understand what he's saying. When I still can't, I furrow my brow. "What?"

"I thought you were hurting yourself," he admits, looking away. He's nervous of what I think? That's the first. Somehow it makes me feel oddly powerful, the fact that I can make him—the infamous Exiled Alpha—nervous.

I laugh, feeling stupid that all of this misery came from one misunderstanding.

"Riot, that was years ago," I assure him, hoping he'll drop the subject in a whole.

"How many years ago?"

"...Okay, one, but that's over. I wasn't—I was just smoking. That's all." I'm in such a hurry to shrink the severity of the situation that my words come out in a stumble.

I can tell he doesn't like the answer. His expression darkens again and his eyes go out of focus. Shit.

"I won't smoke anymore." My voice is unintentionally soft as I stand up from the railing and step toward him.

He nods. "Thank you."

He reaches his hand out toward me. I take it, allowing him to pull me closer. Soon we're so close that I have to adapt by straddling his lap. I smile internally, feeling the warmth between us at his addictive touch.

"If you ever crave it, or feel whatever it is that makes you want it, tell me. Just don't hurt yourself. Do you understand?" His tone is firm yet gentle. Completely different from the one featured in our first conversation about the topic.

I nod, smiling. He meant well before. He just doesn't know what it means to act rationally. When he starts to lean in, I stop him. My palms press against his shoulders, holding him there.

"I would, but I'll taste like an ashtray."

"Shut up," he laughs. With that he pushes easily past the invisible barrier, intentions of pressing his warm lips passionately to mine. I bend down, meeting him halfway.

My nerve endings come alive as my spine tingles with ecstasy. We each growl softly into the kiss. He squeezes the sides of my thighs and pulls me closer as if I'd be jerked away at any second.

Eventually we pull apart, panting. Our foreheads are pressed together, my hair falling down to create a makeshift curtain around our faces. Separating us from the world. How ironic.

I readjust myself to sit sideways on his lap and lay my head on his shoulder. His arms wrap around me protectively, like I'm some kind of prized possession that all the other kids on the playground are trying to touch.

The air is liberatingly cool. Past the edge of the roof I can see the bluish-black sky, starless and bare except for the gibbous moon acting like a nightlight. An owl hoots somewhere nearby, making it all the more whimsical.

This porch is like a safe place. So quiet and peaceful. Maybe it's not so much the porch that makes me feel safe, but rather the neurotic beast clinging to me like a teddy bear.

I look over at Riot. A thin slice of moonlight is shining on his face, illuminating him. If only the world could see him how I do. Maybe then they wouldn't be so willing to drop their life savings for his death.

But then again, I don't know the side they do. Having spent a good portion of my life locked several feet below ground surface for months at a time, current events aren't exactly my best subject.

I wasn't free three years ago to witness the effect or listen to the gossip when he conquered Balaige. But I do remember the way everyone acted when the word of his exile came about. How scared they all were. How utterly panicked. I shudder at the thought of the tyrant on top of the world.

"You're cold?" His concerned voice brings me back to reality.

"No. I'm fine. I like the cold." I answer, snuggling deeper into his side anyway.

I start to drift off, batting my eyes tiredly. The teasing mistress of sleep is back, and she's finally decided to grant me mercy. The last thing I remember before she takes me is Riot carrying me up the stairs and the feel of the cool sheets on my skin.

28 | Blood Of A God

Consciousness comes in the form of Riot's bare chest against my face and his arm wrapped around my torso like a python. I don't bother waking him up. Instead I attempt to gain my freedom by rolling over, which only triggers that aforementioned python to go on lock down.

Through the open curtains on the wall straight in front of me, I can see the blackness of the outside. Dreary and dark.

A crack of thunder rumbles through the house briefly, vibrating the bed gently. Riot nuzzles his nose into my disheveled hair, still asleep. It's as if, even unconsciously, he's showing me that he's still there. I smile before closing my eyes again.

• • •

Morning rolls around and when the sun comes up it stays dark outside. The heavy patter of rain drums on the roof above, creating a relaxing sort of lullaby.

We're both awake now, but neither one of us makes a move to get up. My arm is thrown lazily across his washboard stomach, one leg tangled with his while my temple lays his shoulder. His arm is wrapped around me, making me feel once again safe and sound.

He presses a kiss to my forehead, melting me from the inside out. He has this way of always being intimidating— whether he's threatening the lives of others or putting butterflies in my stomach. The unfairness of the power he has drives me crazy. But maybe that's why it took him so long to accept this; because he feels the same way.

"Are you ready to get up?" His morning voice sends shivers down my back.

I groan. I never want to get up. How many more chances like this will I get? "Do we have to?"

Right then, as if on cue, my stomach decides to recite the symphony of a starving whale, growling unrealistically loud.

"Yes," he chuckles, poking me right above the belly button. He untangles our bodies and sits up. Immediately I feel lost without his added warmth and firm embrace. A pang of vulnerability shoots through me and I quickly knock it down.

From where I'm laying, I catch glimpse of the little black symbol made into his skin. A dire descendant. I know what that mark means and the history of it. But what about the other peculiar thing etched into his flesh?

When he stands up and stretches the muscles of his back glide fluently beneath his skin. I can almost feel my pupils dilate.

"Nooo," I whine and stretch my limbs. I'm not ready to leave this moment yet. And when I reach out for him, he's not long coming back to me. He sits down beside me on the bed, tucking one leg beneath him.

My eyes land on the three long scars running diagonally across his pec. The only other flaw that marks his flawless body. I haven't thought that much about it before. How he got that scar. All I know is that it came from his own hand.

I put my hand overtop of his and raise them both up to his chest. With my fingers overlapping his, I line them up perfectly with the grisly claw mark. It's like putting the missing piece in the last slot of the puzzle.

"Why did you do it?" I ask quietly. There's so many mysteries about this wolf. And I want to know every single one.

He arches an eyebrow, catching my fingers between his and curling them into his palm. "Do you really want to know?"

I nod, certain that I do.

He takes a deep breath, closing his eyes.

"It's from when I left this pack. Almost four years ago," he starts. "Those ear rings, they're permanent right?" He looks at my ear and I nod again. That's common sense. Pack rings don't come out. Ever.

"No they're not," he corrects.

I scrunch my face up. Now he's lost me. There's no possible way to remove a ring once it's in. There's just not. The Bastieelian metal they're made from is unbreakable, and even then they're blessed by our ancestors. They simply don't come out.

"My parents brought us here as rogues. Minutes after stepping through the gates we're being tagged like trophy kills with those goddamn ear rings."

I remember seeing Senya's. The color gold: Khopeski's trademark. She still has hers, but Riot doesn't. His ears are untouched, leaving no possibility that a ring was ever near it.

"You want to know why I hate this place? All of the fucking rules. It's a fine if you so much as breathe the wrong way. I couldn't go anywhere or do anything without half these assholes watching me and the other half telling me what to do. They wanted to smother me."

As he talks, his voice gets increasingly more passionate and angry. Just remembering it is irritating him as if it were over four years ago and he's still living here.

As I think about it, his hatred starts to seem justified. He lived his life as the rogue he was born as and suddenly he's being buried in pack rules and judgmental members. For a wolf who loathes control, his parents had a snowball's chance in hell of that going smoothly.

"And Senya..." I trail off. I have so many questions about her, but I'm scared of asking the wrong one. One sensitive subject and he's liable to lose what rationality he contains.

"She laid down like the perfect lap dog," he growls, "She kissed every ass she possibly could. She even sided with them. She didn't give a fuck what they did, just that they were right and I was wrong."

He throws his arms out to the sides, gesturing to our surroundings. "Look at where we are! This is because she can't stand that I broke the rules and left this hellhole."

I've determined that "they" is anyone in the Khopeski pack, especially anyone with authority. Although I know Riot's anger isn't directed at me, my nerves can't help but to be on edge. He gives off the exact violently unstable air that I've heard whispered about before. Though that's never stopped me before.

"You wanted out," I state softly. There is no comforting for something like this. The least I can do is show that I'm listening.

He nods. "The Hierarchy hates me. When I called them to council to say I was leaving, they refused to let me. If I walked out those gates, I won and they lost. And god forbid that happens," he says sarcastically.

His hand subconsciously squeezes mine with a bone crushing force as he tells the next part. Nonetheless I grit my teeth and hope I don't hear something crack.

"Instinct told me what to do. I have no idea how it worked but it did. I dug until my claws scraped bone, Adrienne. Then the blood did the rest. It fell off and the hole in my ear disappeared."

I squint, baffled beyond comprehension. Blood? Blood doesn't melt metal. It would have to be the blood of a god to do that. Lava would barely even melt Bastieel metal. What he's telling me is far fetched at best and beyond impossible.

But it doesn't even cross my mind to call him a liar.

• • •

I didn't ask anymore questions. I decided that trying my luck to see how angry he could become without breaking something would be a bad idea. So I avoided it, despite the herculean urge to ask about his parents and the story behind what he said to Senya.

"They killed our parents! If you weren't so far up his ass you would realize that!"

They were dead. Anyone could guess that. But it's just the matter of how. I can't imagine what it would be like to lose your parents once you've had them.

My route to becoming an orphan was virtually painless. I didn't know them to grieve them and the underlying resentment that I'd been abandoned only helped me along the way. But Riot was barely a teenager when his were ripped away from him. The people who raised him, taken away by murder. It has to sting.

I comfort Riot in the only way I know how: by touching him. Touch is the only thing that can calm him down, along with a few choice words here and there, which I'm currently out of. So a long lasting hug and a soothing hand rubbing his back will have to suffice for now.

My stomach kept growling afterwords, so eventually Riot insisted we head downstairs to the kitchen.

"Do you know how to cook?" He asks, going through the cabins over the counters.

I laugh. "Honestly? I shouldn't even be allowed in here."

Agatha would be growling in her grave right now, jumping at the chance to put me through misery. I can all but hear her nagging in my ear, saying she's taught me all there is to know and then blaming me when I don't know it.

I'm occupied with irritating memories of the old woman who couldn't break me trying her damnedest at it when Riot turns around. Before I know it, a bowl of white powder, milk, and eggs is being shoved into my hands.

"What are you- No, this is really a bad idea."

He hands me a handheld device with two whisks and an electric cord attached.

"I trust you," he says meaningfully, touching my hand gently.

I raise my eyebrows in amazement. "You truly are self destructive."

With a quick kiss to the top of my head, Riot tells me he has to go pick something up in the city. Before I can protest, he's already out the door. Which means leaving me to my own devices.

A certain inkling tells me that he truly wants this house to burn down. And considering his very blatant hatred of Khopeski, I don't doubt it in the slightest.

Minutes is all I expect it to take before everything spirals out of control, but somehow I surprise even myself. Nothing is burning or broken yet. If Nagatha's cataract blurred vision could see me now she might even be proud.

That's what I would like to think at least. In reality it would be a lecture about the proper method of stirring.

God, I want a cigarette.

So maybe the kitchen hasn't gone up in flames yet, but at what cost? It takes effort, which only gives back stress in return. Everything is beeping— the oven, the microwave, and whatever other appliance I've forgotten to turn off.

It's gone to my head. I can hear the ringing in my ears, multiplying in my imagination.

Why does he hate me? Haven't I paid enough for the train incident?

Why would anyone put themselves through this? Our ancestors had the right idea. I would rather eat a raw carcass than go through this, too.

Out of the corner of my eye, though the thick silk curtains, a shadow moves.

It's the beeping. It's driving me mad.

Then, through the crackling of bacon and blaring of timers, I hear something. A sudden shattering coming from the back patio.

The chance to leave the kitchen and all of the beeping behind is a golden opportunity I can't pass up. My senses tingle in alertness the closer I get to the glass door with the shades drawn. Whatever is on the other side, my wolf instincts don't have a good feeling about.

I jerk the door open to find nothing but a clay pot shattered on the ground, the plant and its soil strewn across the patio.

As soon as my foot crosses the threshold of the house, my mistake is confirmed. An arm loops around my neck, dragging me backwards into a body.

"GET OFF, YOU FU-"

A rag smashes against my face. The smell of chemicals smothers me.

My vision tunnels, caving in. The last thing I pick up on is that goddamn beeping. Except it's more high pitched. More shrill and annoyingly persistent. Like a smoke detector.

29 | Shattering Screams

Cold stone against my skin. Ropes tied tightly around my wrists. Those are the first things to welcome me back into consciousness. I sit up, bones popping with stiffness.

I recognize with a stab of trepidation the face sitting only yards away: Romanov. He's sitting cross legged across the room, staring at me with the intensity of a scorned animal. His face is unreadable, yet somehow I can read it just fine, having had plenty of practice with Riot. I have an idea as to why I'm here, but I don't want to believe it as true.

"She's awake!" Romanov calls, not breaking eye contact for even a second, "Bring him in."

While we wait in silence for "him" to arrive, I take the chance to stake out my surroundings. The room is large and circular, with floors and walls made of cobblestone. The ceiling comes to a hollow point above in the shape of a turret. Small windows dot the walls, like that of a medieval watch tower. Outside the windows the sky is a dark gray, an abyss of angry storm clouds brewing over the white and gold city. Rain drizzles down heavily, so dark that you can hardly tell it's day instead of night.

At the side of the room it begins to square off into a descending stairwell. From that stairwell comes a boy, every piece of his apparel black and every part of his body leaden with a weapon sheathe. One feature jumps out at me with a chill, and those are the dead eyes in his skull that are fixed on the ground, void of emotion.

Something oblong and large is draped over his shoulder. It's wrapped in black plastic and looks eerily life-sized. He drops it carelessly on the ground beside me. It lands with a dull with a thud. Romanov gets up and the bounty hunter he'd called in steps back. With a gloved hand, Romanov pulls away a portion of the plastic.

I cringe, the rancid stench of decaying flesh burning my nostrils. The corpse's skin is pale. His eyes are still open, staring hauntingly up at ceiling. They're glazed over, the expression of fear frozen inside them. Half of his face is completely gone, torn off down to the dirty white of the bone. His jaw is slack, only a slither of flesh holding it together.

"Do you recognize him?" Romanov asks, almost accusingly. This is why I'm here? To play guessing games for the name to a mound of mutilated flesh?

"How could I? He barely has a face," I say, my palm muffling my words.

Romanov growls, apparently displeased with my answer. "Smell again. Closer."

"Sniffing the dead isn't really my thing-"

"NOW!" He barks, shoving my head next to the dead man's.

I only stop recoiling when realization hits me like a ton of bricks. The color drains from my face, just like his did.

The blood that Riot came back covered in smells exactly the same as the blood dried to this corpse's torn and flayed flesh.

This is the hunter from last night. The spy that snapped one too many twigs in the bushes. Of course that's why I'm here. Romanov made it very clear; if Riot breaks any law, any at all, then this entire deal is over. Possibly along with other things, such as my life.

For once, I hate the fact that I'm right.

This is him. And his is what Riot done to him. He ripped him apart. Dissected him like a frog. And now I have to answer for it. For letting the tyrant "run off leash."

Romanov must notice my pale face and gaping jaw, though not as pale and gaping as his friend I'm sure. He bends down and throws the plastic blanket back over the body.

"He's only the first of many I've found in the last 24 hours. So maybe you'd like to tell me why my hunters are dropping like flies." He steps threateningly closer and I scoot cautiously back.

His fist lunges forward, grabbing the portion of rope between my hands and yanking me to my feet. My eyes are wide and my heart is thumping mercilessly in my chest. A strand of feather-light hair falls across the bridge of my nose as I'm held face to face with the mercenary hired to kill my mate. I'm so close that I can see every one of the pores in his skin and each singular hair that makes up his beard.

I shake my head, not trusting myself to answer and keep my throat un-slit.

His hand shoots up, gripping my jaw with an iron claw. He tilts my head up, squeezing tighter as if with a vengeance.

"I told you to keep him under control," he snarls through gritted teeth. His dark eyes are hot, boiling in fact. He spits his words at me like they're venom capable of burning me. "I agreed to this fucking deal because that's what Senya wanted. And now nobody's happy, all because you couldn't do your fucking part."

Guilt fills my stomach. Romanov is right. I had a part, one given to me through menace and warning, but I had a part nonetheless. One that I didn't fulfill.

Why did I let Riot leave? I should have kept him with me. I should have made sure his claws stayed fingernails and his canines teeth.

But I didn't. I'm not his keeper. So why the hell am I feeling guilty over this?

Then I realize what Romanov's doing. He's manipulative. He's the kind of person whom controlling others comes easily to. Somehow it reminds of Senya, which makes all the more sense. I have an inkling that they're close, meaning it's only logical that they be alike in some ways.

"Then don't.. send people.. to watch us," I wheeze out, the heel of his hand crushing my throat.

"I'll do whatever I want," he seethes, "There was no agreement against that."

I have his attention. I can't afford to lose it. It may be my hopeful imagination, but I think I hear a microscopic slither of defense in his voice. Actually, I'm certain that I did.

I squirm against his hold until it's loose enough to breathe.

"You wanted this to happen," I accuse bitterly, "You know what sets him off. And you know that surveillance is one of them. You just wanted to make killing him easier on your conscious."

"I don't give a shit about his petty little temperament issues or his life."

I shrug my shoulders nonchalantly. "You may not, but Senya does."

I remember what Riot told me about his life in Khopeski and how much he hated being watched by the townspeople. The more I think about it, the more I'm sure of myself, and the more I'm sure that Romanov had a plan all along.

"If you at all value your hunters' lives as much as you claim to," I jab a finger blindly towards the covered corpse, "Then you wouldn't have sent someone as easy to find as he was. If that's how all you train all of them then it's no wonder you're so eager to cash in on Riot's bounty. That's a ridiculous price considering the poor service the people are getting back."

It's as if as soon as I'm done we both remember his hand on my neck. I take a gulp of breath right before he reestablishes his crushing hold as a punishment.

Bastard is the only word I can think of as I feel my face reddening and my lungs screaming for air.

My vision starts to blur and distort, black splotches appearing at the sides. My head starts spinning at the lack of oxygen.

Then, screams shatter the air. A multitude of them, bloodcurdling and terrified. I can't tell if it's hallucination or reality. Romanov's grip lets up. It takes a minute for my eyesight to return.

His head is turned, senses alert to listen. I don't question it. My mind is running so fast that it' freezes in place and instincts take over as compensation.

With a hard shove, I break away from Romanov. In a flash I'm bent over, sawing at the bindings on my ankles and wrists with sharpened claws. The rope severs within seconds.

I stand up just in time for a hard fist to connect with my cheek. It knocks my head sideways and forces a sharp pain through my lip, my teeth undoubtedly slicing it open. Pain pulses through my face, but the time to process it is a luxury I can't afford.

Fear and adrenaline drive me to the only conclusion I find reasonable. My body shifts into a cream colored wolf and with a roaring snarl I lunge at Romanov. His back slams into the stone with great satisfaction, my weight driving him further into it. Almost immediately his hands curl around my snout, slamming my snapping jaws shut. I retaliate by clawing at his chest, tearing his shirt and digging down into the bloody flesh.

From the corner of my eye, the other hunter is running towards us. I leap off of Romanov's writhing body before either of them can pin me down.

Using my experience with Senya as an indicator, I quickly choose flight over fight. Bounty hunters don't play fair, and melting my skin off a second time isn't present on my list of ambitions.

I dive head first down the winding staircase, towards whatever waits for me at the bottom. It's only midway down when I make a sickening realization, and that's that I'm running straight towards the sound of the screaming. And it's anything but a hallucination.

Outside of the tower, the rain pounds down with intentions of shattering the cobblestone streets. Anxiety rises in my gut, giving me the desire to hurl as I come to a sudden halt. I'm trapped in a terrifying vortex of panic. Behind me is a man who wants me dead and in front of me are the ear piercing shrieks of an entire city thrown into chaos.

I make my decision and gamble with my chances. Out of the shelter of the tower entrance, the downpour immediately soaks my fur, making my pelt ten times heavier. But I keep on, sprinting through the streets despite the thunder shaking the ground. Despite the high pitched wailing rising too close for comfort, only three streets away.

A shiver of alertness shocks my heart. There's nothing like the expression of vocalized horror in a throat-tearing cry to send your nerves over the edge. Not to mention what sounds like hundreds of them.

Damn this city!

There are so many twists and turns and pointless detours solely for the purpose of decor or extravagance. I trot to a stop at a fountain in a lavishly designed circular plaza that I've never seen before. Fuckkkk.

The array of screaming is coming closer. Eerily in a way that sounds like the people are being herded. No. Herded isn't the word for it. Chased.

My chest heaves for air, my fur completely soaked. Hysteria makes every-thing worse. The pounding in my ears. The spastic beating of my heart. Where is the goddamn exit?! Indecision clouds my thoughts. All I know is that I want out of this place— this prison—that I'm in.

I sense hyperventilation coming just as my breathing jars and accelerates.

Find peace. Just find peace.

I start thinking of the forests. Of the fresh air, of the silence, and of the freedom. I close my eyes in an attempt to pull myself back together.

Suddenly I'm back walking in the forest by Riot's cabin. I remember the chill of the air, the quiet sun painting the sky an array of soft colors.

And then I remember what happened next.

I'm thrown harshly back into reality when a giant weight drops down on my back. Deja vu that's all too real.

30 | Ruby Red Eyes

A snarl rips from my throat as I thrash wildly, trying to throw my attacker off. The movements are so familiar that it feels like a flashback I can't snap out of.

A thick arm slides around my neck like a noose. A hand grabs my snout, attempting with great effort to twist my head sideways. After all, a broken neck would be quicker than strangulation.

I come to a sudden stop and flip over on the cobblestone like I'm trying to put out a fire. The air is crushed out of the monkey on my back, causing their hold to break just long enough for me to slip out. I don't take my opportunity for granted, making quick work of pinning the attacker down.

I find myself staring into the eyes of Romanov, their icy irises paradoxically burning with rage. My paw finds its place against his neck, the tips of my claws just barely entering his skin. I curl my lips back in a snarl.

I had expected to see some form of fear cross his face. A bit of uncertainty at the least. But his air of arrogance and anger doesn't falter.

"Shift back," he demands, though demands aren't usually made by the one on the ground.

Or what? I want to ask him. But he saves me the trouble because it's like he reads my mind. Something pokes my underbelly, a sharp, fine point. A needle.

"Unless you want another dose of Senya's silverbane." There's the threat I had been anticipating. The reason why he let himself get pinned so quickly. He has a secret weapon he knows I won't oppose.

A vile memory pops into my head. How badly it hurt when Senya drenched me in it. The sheer pain and acid-like burning as the liquid ate straight through my flesh and down to the bone, along with the nauseating feeling that followed. I don't want another taste of that, whatever the hell it is.

With a baleful glare, I slowly step off of him. The more I encounter of this bastard, the more I hate him. I loathe every single particle of air that has ever kept him alive.

"Now shift," he barks. He's to his feet now, wielding a syringe full of a metallic, silver substance. His thumb is poised on the plunger, ready to make good on his threat.

I trade my pride for logic and do as he says. My bones crack and realign. Sinewy fibers stretch and pull back together in new positions. Seconds later and I'm standing with humility heating my face. I fight the urge to cover the burn scars, covering my private parts instead.

I open my mouth, a slew of curses right at the top of my tongue. Somewhere nearby, a horrifying scream rings out, jolting me. Except this time it's not only screams. A monstrous roar echoes, so powerful that the very core of the city shakes.

It's close. Painfully, terrifyingly close. It's like an electric pulse shoots through my brain. My senses are dulled yet very much alive. Pounding footfalls approaching behind me, charging rapidly. At the last minute, intuition controls my body.

With a rolling leap to the side, I make it out of the way just in time. Seconds later comes the thick impact of flesh meeting flesh.

I snap my head over to look. A giant wolf is standing over Romanov's body, plowed into the concrete by the impact. Its dark fur is spiky and wet from the rain, the hairs bristled to a point on its back.

Riot.

I watch, speechless, at what unfolds a few meters away from me. Riot's canines sink into Romanov's shoulder right before he's turned into a life-sized rag doll. My eyes are widen like saucers as I observe.

Romanov is flung across the plaza as if he were weightless. Threads scream as his shirt is clamped in Riot's jaws, fabric tearing as its wear is sent slamming into the ground.

In that head jerking movement, I catch a flash of Riot's eyes. It turns my blood cold.

Red. A flash of glowing, ruby red.

My heart throbs in my throat until I swallow it back down.

He's lost control...

A ripple of panic surges through me like an unrelenting tidal wave. I've only seen those eyes twice before. The fourth and final stage. The eyes that incite raw terror in their onlookers no matter how brave you are. The eyes that raise a survival hysteria within you, building and building until you break and the predator takes its prey. The eyes of a dire wolf's descendent.

Thunder cracks simultaneously, as if to deliver that very omen of ill will.

Riot's wolf is at the surface and its out for blood— the very thing that now splatters all of the gold in Khopeski.

Romanov crashes into the street, impossibly cracking the stone pathway. He bounces back to his feet with a slight stagger. Crimson streaks run down his partially bare chest, soaking into the torn fabric. In the blink of an eye, his form takes that of a wolf, his fur a hint blacker than that of his opponent's.

The two beasts clash again, this time in a more equal match. The vicious snarls and barks drown out the dull roar of the storm. A voice at the back of my head nags me to get off my ass and do something, but I remain frozen in place. It would be suicide with a loathing if anyone stepped foot in front of that monster.

It goes on like this for half an eternity. Claws and teeth drawing blood and potential death bliss being traded like cards. I want it to end so badly.

Clumps of fur scatter across the ground, mixing with blood and rain.

A shrill whimper breaks above the rest of the noise. The kind of whimper that makes your stomach drop due to the finality of it.

The fighting has stopped. Amidst the rain bouncing off the street lays one of the wolves. Its dark fur blurs its shape. I take a shaky step forward, hesitant.

The smell of blood is weak in the air, diluted by the rainfall. The smell of Riot's, however, is what makes my cry catch in my throat.

He stands above Romanov's body, Riot in human form now. Scarlet streams roll down his back, looking more like weakly dyed water rather than blood. A giant lump of flesh is missing from his shoulder blade. Where the hole is, is a grisly, gaping bite mark.

I resist running to him. Everything worried thought my wolf is screaming at me is drowned out by other things cluttering my head. Uncertainty. Awe. Fright. Disbelief. But most out of all, curiosity. Because he doesn't look like he's done just yet.

He kneels down beside Romanov's canine shape, rolling him onto his back. I'm surprised when his seemingly dead body comes to life, clawing and kicking at Riot with frantic ferocity. While his body writhes, his head never moves. It's as if he's been strapped down from the shoulders up.

A broken neck. How ironic.

The bastard tried to snap mine twice within the hour. A part of me is pleased to discover that karma is so petty. Though another part tells me that karma had nothing to do with it.

I watch unwaveringly as Riot, with a clawed hand, reaches forward and flicks his wrist at the base of each of his foe's limbs. Oddly in a slicing motion. Directly afterwards, Romanov stops struggling.

Then, Riot's hands move to his enemy's chest. I can't look away, nor can I hide the shock on my face.

He claws his way through the pelt, through the flesh, and through the very cage of bones meant to prevent this. As he does this, Romanov's mouth opens wide as if to scream in agony, but nothing comes out.

Riot reaches forearm-deep into Romanov's chest. He murmurs something as he does. Though I can barely hear it, I shudder at the pure hatred dripping off each syllable.

"I'll give it to my sister. She can watch it rot."

He suddenly jerks his hand back, setting off a shower of blood spewing from Romanov's torso.

Riot's hand is painted crimson. Stained and dripping. In his palm is the very thing that life revolves around, the most vital of organs.

In his hand, is Romanov's heart. A distorted, oval shaped lump of tissue and valves, leaking blood like a waterfall.

It hits the stone with a callous thud, landing beside it's owner.

I can do nothing but stare at Riot. His entire body is flawed with various gashes and bites, claw marks and wounds still bleeding. My chest aches at the sight— though I'm sure not nearly as much as Romanov's does.

My eyes meet those of the monster bathed in blood. My breath catches in my throat.

There they are, those ruby red eyes glowing like demonic candles in the hapless night.

The aura they give off makes me want to run. To cower and scream until the nightmares go away. But I'm not scared. In fact, I'm the complete opposite of scared. A sense of pride swells in my chest.

That's my mate.

He's capable of all this. He's a savage killer, an infamous tyrant, and a rogue as heartless as an inanimate object. Yet by some miracle, I get to live on his good side. It's a privilege I'll never lower from the pedestal I hold it on.

As he approaches, I don't move a muscle. I stand perfectly still as he embraces me, wrapping his arms around my shoulders and pulling me into his mauled chest. I try to avoid hitting any of his wounds, but it's physically impossible. Instead of wincing, he breathes a sigh of relief.

He pulls away to inspect my throat, gently turning my head side to side as if he were a doctor checking for swollen tonsils. It's then that I'm sure my guess was correct. Romanov's broken neck wasn't simply a coincidence after all.

Once he's satisfied with what he sees— no bruises or even a trace of a hand having ever been there— he gives a small growl of approval.

I feel like I should speak or say something, anything, but no words come. His black irises are still present, the red glow still illuminating them.

The rain lets up, lightning streaking through the sky.

"We should go," Riot says, running the pad of his thumb along my jaw. He's never been so soft before. It's like he's afraid I'll crumple at his touch. I nod, remaining speechless. What is there to say? After what I just witnessed, silence seems appropriate.

As soon as I look up, I realize we have an audience. The streets branching off from the circular plaza are swarmed with citizens. They all stare at us, their mouths gaping widely. All of their eyes are unblinking, disbelieving. I study their expressions further, expecting to find fear and distress. Instead I find their faces surprisingly blank, landing somewhere between shock and awe.

31 | If We're Lucky

At the head of one street is a group of bounty hunters— trademarked by their sinister black apparel and deadly tools strapped to every body part. They stand out from the rest of the crowd for more reasons than their clothing. They're visibly distraught.

The first expression they've ever portrayed in front of an audience, and it's one of grief. The hunters' shoulders are slumped, gloved fists balled at their sides. Some of their mouths are twitching, lips quivering as they try, in great effort, to keep the poker faces they were trained to.

Rather than going into a blind rage from looking upon their leader's dead body, they seem... shattered.

Romanov was their kingpin while they were just numbers under his control. That's what I had thought at least. Looking at them now, standing frozen in place with shock, maybe I was wrong.

Senya...

She's a bounty hunter just as they are, but her distressed-tinged face isn't among them. She isn't here and the leaden feeling spreading in my stomach tells me that's a good thing.

"Riot," I dare cautiously, "We need to go. Now."

He doesn't respond. My mate is standing just as statue-still as the bounty hunters staring at us across the diameter of the plaza. Except his countenance is achieving exactly what the hunters would covet: a cold, unreadable expression.

It's as I look between the two opposing parties that I realize I'm not the one being stared at. Just like the punishments back in Visari, my presence isn't even acknowledged. No. They're staring at the wolf standing tall beside me, poised and ready to achieve his bloody feat all over again. He remains stoic-faced, despite a whole city's worth of werewolves' eyes staying glued on him. The same eyes of the people he's expressed so much hatred for.

In front of all of us, his ruby red eyes start to fade. The red glow dies out, leaving obsidian irises surging with wisps of deep grey, like a monochrome fire burning inside them.

He's unaffected by the attention, completely emotionless. Possibly even a bit disdainful. It's the exact same demeanor he carried in Visari, and undoubtedly the same he had when he dominated Balaige.

And with it, he turns and walks away.

• • •

Never did I think I'd be so relieved to be sitting back in this giant hunk of iron and steel ever again. This time the train car is empty of anyone else but us. The night hours, Riot explained, aren't as popular among humans.

With a heavy sigh, I let myself sink down into the cushioned seat, for some reason thinking that it might be able massage away the reality of it all.

"Exiled" isn't a strong enough word to describe what Riot is anymore. Nor are the thousands of death warrants on his head enough to describe his public image.

I followed Riot out of the city as if we were going on a casual stroll. He was as calm as a dead man while I was an overly anxious bundle of nerves waiting for a flaming arrow to stick into his back. When we approached the golden gates, the guards took one glance at the bloody wolf accompanying me and opened them without question. It was as if the news of Romanov's death had spread without a word.

Everyone feared the Exiled Alpha before. The whispers of the things he's done at Balaige made sure of that. Now it's like they're scared in a different way. As if they know now that it isn't the title of 'Alpha' that he's after. And if they don't, I do.

If he killed Romanov Lashveiska, the very man nearly ten thousand people turned to to trust in bringing the tyrant's death, then this is the end. There is no one else. There's no other being left to bring him down.

Riot Sydney has come out on top. They all know that.

The very wolf whose name is known across the werewolf world is sitting a mere foot away from me, leaning back in the seat with his eyelids closed.

"Riot?"

"Hm?" He doesn't open his eyes.

"What was Romanov like?"

"You met the bastard. You should know." He crosses his arms and slides further down into his seat, unfazed by the question. But I've caught on to him. Everything he does is the opposite of what he thinks. It bothers him, the mention of that name even though its owner is dead.

"You wanna know what I think of him?" I pull my legs up under myself, trying try to act like there's not a punchline dancing on the tip of my tongue.

He opens one eye as if to ask what?

"I think he's heartless." I barely get the words out before my lips crack into a smile and I suppress my childish laughter.

Riot closes his one open eyelid again and lets his head fall backward. He exhales heavily through his nose, telling me just how disappointed he is better than words ever could. But his mouth curls into a grin anyway.

Soon I let my laughter out and he joins me. He drags his hand down his face as he quietly chuckles to himself.

"I hate you." He murmurs, though he looks over at me in a way that says just the opposite.

I offer him a cheeky smile. "I know."

• • •

After a handful of hours nodding off on the train, I'm reminded of how long and miserable the ride back home is. At least this time there are no humans around to inebriate my senses.

We get off the train at a different location than where we had boarded with Senya. At the sight of the unfamiliar surroundings, I'm fully prepared to let another wave of panic set in. Riot, thankfully, seems to know where we are.

With a gentle yet confident hand on my back, he leads us away from the asphalt of human society and back into the woods my wolf has been calling for. The smell of nature— dirt, leaves, trees, and even the air itself— comforts me.

I was so sick of that city. It had a unique sense of undeniable beauty to it and was extravagant in every sense of the word, but there's toxins in the ground. The longer I stayed there, the more I started to understand Riot's hatred for the place.

• • •

Another couple of hours was spent walking through the forest on no designated path. Eventually the trees started to become vaguely familiar; the place where I never got to finish my morning walk before being attacked by a blackmailing bounty hunter. The memory makes a question pop into my head.

"Do you think we'll see Senya again?" I ask Riot, looking over to where he strides along beside me. He seems lost in his thoughts.

"Not if we're lucky." There's no trace of humor in his cold voice. He was a lot funner when he actually tried laughing. It takes a hefty amount of willpower to resist the urge to tell him that.

A spike of excitement hits me when the cabin comes into view over the ridge. I notice Riot come to a stop behind me.

"You go ahead," he says, looking back in the way we came. His shoulders are tense and he seems distracted. He's been like that the entire trip here, though I've intentionally ignored it in attempt to give him space.

"They didn't follow us," I assure him, "We even took a different route." There's no way in hell any of those people who witnessed what I did would dare follow the same trail as Riot. I'm confident of that.

"I have to make sure." With that he turns and disappears between the trees. I roll my eyes and continue toward the cabin.

By the time I reach the bottom of the small ridge, the darkness has become more prominent. Night is falling, casting shadows among the ground and dimming the sky.

With a pang of trepidation ricocheting in my stomach, I see the sliding glass door of the kitchen standing wide open. My senses kick into high alert, goosebumps prickling along my arms. The hair on the back of my neck stands on end as I approach the open door.

The inside of the cabin is a pitch black abyss of shadows. I stall for a few seconds, waiting for my eyes to adjust to the dark. I ease through the house, subconsciously holding my breath to listen for even the faintest sounds of someone else's breathing.

In the middle of the living room, a chill runs down my spine. A scent is lingering ever so faintly in the air. A reluctantly familiar scent that makes me want to vomit.

Nathan.

That narcissistic asshole was in this house, his grimy hands pawing all over everything. The thought makes me want to light a match and thrown it down.

Why was he here? It's been weeks since our last encounter, surely he's moved on from his delusion by now.

What I find odd is that Nathan's is the only scent here. There's no trace of anyone else, no pack members that might have been drug along with him to ambush us. He came alone.

He really is an idiot.

After a quick trip around the entire cabin, I'm irked to find his smell in every single room. I quickly start opening windows and doors, waving papers as fans and trying my best the air the place out before Riot arrives.

I remember all too well how he reacts whenever anything about Nathan is mentioned. He hates his guts more than Romanov's, possibly even more than the entirety of the Khopeski pack combined.

If Riot picks up his trail here, I'm afraid he won't stop until he follows him all the way back to Visari. Ripping Romanov's heart out was one thing. His hunters were too grief stricken and shocked to react. But if Nathan somehow ends up with a morbid death, the story won't be the same.

Alpha Andre isn't the grieving type. He prefers revenge instead.

Out an open window in the corner of my eye, I see Riot's figure approaching. Sprinting down the stairs as fast as I can and nearly wiping out at the bottom, I manage to reach the back door just as he's about to come in.

"Hey," I greet, only slightly breathlessly as I place myself in front of the doorway. "Find anyone?"

He shakes his head before looking at me suspiciously. "Why are you out of breath?"

Damn him.

"I fell on the stairs just now." Which isn't totally a lie. "Don't worry about it. I'm fine."

He seems to accept the answer as he goes to take a step inside. Immediately I block his path, masking the action by slipping my arms under his and turning it into a hug.

Once again I earn the same suspicious expression as his eyes scrape over me and around the inside of the house.

"Why are the windows open?" Despite the suspicion, he absentmindedly returns my hug.

Like a slow motion football tackle, I push him further out the door as I answer, "There was a musty smell." Once again, not a lie. "Come sit with me on the porch."

He stops me dead in my tracks, like a boulder not about to move another inch.

The length of his index finger under my chin forces my gaze up to him. His, however, is locked on my lips.

"Gladly," he says before softly pressing his mouth to mine.

32 | The Visarian Way

Lighting the fireplace, I watch the flames burst from the tinder. Dim orange light flickers on the walls, parting the darkness like the Red Sea. I sit cross legged on the floor, staring into the fire as if it would somehow bring peace. My eyes go out of focus, the colors of the room blurring together.

The Exiled Alpha: so famous, yet so unknown. So feared and hated, yet simultaneously respected. He toppled an entire pack single handedly. He cut them off from the world and kept it that way for three years until they finally exiled him.

"How did he do it?" Is what every werewolf across the globe has asked at least once. I'm mated to him and even I still don't know. Although I have some theories.

Having witnessed his rampage through the pack of Khopeski, the terrible screams are still stuck in my ears. Never have I felt the same terror and dread as I do when catching glimpse of those ruby red eyes.

A dire descendent. That's the biggest mystery about him. There's no doubt that it ties closely into his personality; his impulsivity, the reasoning behind what makes him tick.

What does make him tick?

He was born a rogue and remains one at heart. Rebellion is in his blood as much as his feral ancestors are. Any type of control is a massive set off just asking for a consequence, the only question being how many.

So what drove him to overtake a pack if he hates them so much?

The answer is simple: because he could. He felt controlled in Khopeski, judged and suffocated. He felt betrayed by his family for taking him out of the woods and throwing him into a cesspool of rules and laws and expecting him to lie down. So that was his statement: he makes the rules.

Two legs wrap around mine from either side, joined by a pair of arms wrapping around my torso from behind. My back is pulled close against a solid chest, fitting into the contour of another body.

My skin prickles at the warming sensation of his touch and the inviting sense of his embrace.

Riot's forehead comes to lay on my shoulder, his nose nuzzling into my neck. The hot breath and scolding mouth make me shiver as if it were the dead of winter.

I lean into him, dreading the thought of running damage control for the nth time.

"Is your wolf coming up again?" I ask with a tone that's trained for the occasion, sweet-tempered but firm. A flare-up is the last thing I need right now. I'm too exhausted to put up with another episode from him and his wolf. If only he would stop fighting.

"No," he murmurs into my neck.

Realization hits like a cold mist. He stopped resisting his instincts a long time ago. There are no more tormented fits or internal turmoil. It must be something about being back in this house that made my mind go back to before.

I remember the first time I met Riot— when he crashed a narcissist's plans for a blackmailed wedding— and how awfully we got along. A pang of giddiness shoots through me at realizing how different it is now. How he's draped over me like a protective blanket instead of tying me up like a prisoner.

Life does get better.

Hot tears spring to my eyes. I quickly blink them away, silently laughing at myself for being so absurdly sappy. I'm so ecstatic that pressure is building in my chest, ready to burst into a laughing hysteria any moment.

I lay back, resting my head on Riot's shoulder. I look over at him. His warm copper eyes hold something bright and entrancing.

"I want to mark you." His voice is husky.

My stomach tightens. It sounds so final. So serious. But I break out into a grin anyway. "So mark me."

Razor sharp canines graze my skin, starting to pinch down.

"Wait!" I shout, a little too abruptly, as I jerk away from him. His eyes immediately darken, the rare copper color disappearing under an evading oil spill. Quickly, I put out the fire before it can start. "Not the neck."

His spark of premature rage fizzles into confusion, brows furrowing. "Then where?"

"The Visarian way."

This only confuses him more. "I thought they were dead to you?" He asks, tiling his head slightly.

"The people are. My culture isn't," I answer simply. The green metallic ring in my ear holds true as my birthright. No matter what Nathan does to that pack, I know who I am.

"I'll show you." I spin around, positioning myself to face him at an intimately close proximity.

I reach over and take hold of the collar of his shirt, gently tugging it upward. With a devilish smirk he takes the hint. In a matter of seconds the shirt is off and, coincidentally, thrown on top of my head. Even at such a crucial moment he still has to be a pain.

With a playful growl, the shirt gets tossed aside.

"We mark below the neck, not quite on the shoulder; here at the upper trapezius," I run my finger tip over the raised and sculpted muscle connecting his neck to his shoulder.

"We both mark?"

I nod and wait for his reaction. A lot of wolves hate the idea of a two way marking because it's not "traditional." Even in the tribal packs' ancestry, there's evidence of two way markings having taken place. But some people choose to stay ignorant. People like Agatha.

Riot's expression, however, doesn't change. It's as if the difference doesn't phase him in the slightest.

His large hands take my sides and pull me into his lap. I compensate by wrapping my legs around around his abdomen.

He then leans his head to the side and stretches his neck out, allowing me better access. His skin all but glows in the firelight, like a god presenting himself to a mortal. He looks as though he were cast from a one-of-a-kind mold, built to demolish an opposer with one swing. What irks me even further is that even his flaws are attractive. It's damn near impossible to focus on the task at hand.

With an extreme burst of willpower, I rip my eyes away long enough to press my lips against his trapezius. My canines protrude out from my gums, my wolf already aware of what's happening.

I place my palms his biceps in order to stabilize him. And then, pulling my lips back, my lengthened teeth slowly sink into his flesh and muscle.

His hot blood fills my mouth and I'm immediately filled with remorse. I try to ignore it, to push the guilty thoughts that result from hurting my mate out of my head. I close my eyes, trying to focus on how soft his skin is to my tongue, but instead find myself making notes of my how sinewy it is to sink my teeth into.

He lets out a deep, throaty moan in my ear. His fingers dig into me, holding me tighter and taking fistfuls of my shirt in his hands. It's like a heatwave flashes through the entire room. Or maybe it's the fire from the fireplace spreading and we're just too preoccupied to notice.

After I'm certain it's deep enough to scar, I retract my canines pull away. I make a move to sit back and I'm instantly slammed against him, as if I were going to leave and never come back.

I giggle curtly at how possessive the mark has already made him. On the bright side, at least he doesn't act in pain.

"Did it hurt?"

"Is that a serious question?"

A drop of his blood trickles down my chin. I wipe it away with my sleeve, feeling somewhat ashamed to have harmed him, even though for a normal reason.

Without saying anything else, I reach up to pull my shirt off. Once it's over my head I hesitate, remembering what sullies my stomach. Nervously, I keep the piece of white fabric in my lap, trying as casually as possible to keep the hideous burn marks covered.

He reaches over and silently plucks the shirt away, tossing it to land in a pile with his.

The razor sharp tips of his canines graze my shoulder in the same spot as mine did his. They linger around for bit, as if trying to find the exact placement.

Then, burning pain shoots through me, running all the way to my toes and stemming from where his teeth dig into the flesh. I drag my claws over his arms, fighting the urge to sink them into him as a reaction toward the pain.

Within a millisecond, agony changes into pure pleasure. My entire body comes alive as if an I.V. just got inserted in my wrist and is pumping me full of artificial adrenaline and feel-good drugs. Every nerve ending buzzes and there's a swirling mixture of hot and cold inside me.

It feels like it's over just as quickly as it started, at least a full minute of his teeth biting through my skin and muscle. I know he's gone far enough when the area pulses strongly even after he's pulled away.

He looks just as dazed as I feel. Crimson is smeared across his lips, his tongue darting out to lick them clean.

"Now you're stuck with me for good," I joke, giving him a small shove.

"Lucky me," he replies, overly sarcastic, as he leans forward to plant a kiss on my lips.

We sit in the floor for a while longer, staring blearily into the dancing flames of our cozy little fire.

I yawn loudly, which makes him yawn, which makes me yawn again, which makes him yawn again, which creates a vicious cycle of yawning and burning, blinking eyes.

Finally, he lifts us both to our feet. With his hand on the small of my back, I'm gently nudged in the direction of the stairs.

"Go to bed. I'll put the fire out."

I don't object. I can barely keep my eyelids open at this point and dragging my worn out body up the stairs is hard enough as it is. I enter Riot's room and all but throw myself into the bed. I pull the covers up to my neck and wrap them tightly around me.

Despite the pleasure while getting it, the new mark is insanely tender. I jerk when my hand accidentally hits it, but it doesn't stop me from getting comfortable.

I don't think it's even a full minute before my eyelids become too heavy to stay awake. They close again and this time I don't have the will power to open them back up.

The dip of the bed stirs me into a half-alert awareness when Riot crawls in. He gathers my seemingly lifeless body up in one arm and pulls me against his broad chest, keeping the comforter wrapped tightly around me as I had fixed it.

A kiss is planted on my ear; a silent 'goodnight.'

Subconsciously, I burrow further into him, finding the sense of safe and sound there that I didn't know I've been craving.

-

33 | He Threatened You

Early the next morning, I wake up in a mass of tangled blankets and ruffled pillows. Besides myself, the bed is otherwise empty. The spot where Riot's body used to lay is bare.

Where could he have gone this early? There's barely even a slither of daylight outside and his pillow has long gone cold.

Whatever. He's not my responsibility. He can take care of himself.

After a long, satisfying stretch, I get up with a yawn. My shoulder is sore where Riot's teeth had sank into it and my shirt is encrusted with brown, dried blood. I probably should have changed before going to bed, but I didn't have the energy to even think about it.

I peel it off, discard it to the floor, and replace it with another long sleeve one with blue arms and shoulders and a white body.

While my shirt was off, I caught sight of the mark in the corner of my eye. Scabby, red, and with a few areas still oozing blood. It'll scar over soon enough and become the mark that it's intended to be: a symbol that ties me to Riot. And his will do exactly the same.

Downstairs there's still no sign of him. His scent lingers faintly throughout the cabin, more than enough for me to track through the living room, down the hallway and out the back door.

Against the wall by the door I find my favorite tall grey boots, the ones I was wearing when Riot took me from my pack. It seems like it happened eons ago, a distant memory that I remember vividly.

I slip them on and head out the door, my sense of smell guiding me. Riot's scent trails off into the forest, in a direction I've never bothering going before. I've always been in the woods in front of and to the right of the cabin. Now I'm heading diagonally behind it, with only my nose to lead me.

Dead leaves crunch under my boots, the towering trees looking naked without them. The sky is just beginning to turn a bright blue, although the whole world looks a bit dim with the sun barely peaking over the horizon. There's an autumn chill in the crisp air with a rejuvenating bite to it.

After a little while, not having even walked that terribly far from the cabin, I spot Riot ahead. His back is to me and he's sitting on a stump in a small little clearing among the trees. I notice his shoulders and head hanging lowly, dejectedly. He seems focused on something in front of him.

He hears my footsteps as I approach, his back muscles tensing. But he doesn't raise his head, nor show any blatant sign or acknowledgement of my arrival. When I'm close enough to see over his shoulder, my heart drops at what's holding his attention.

Two graves, side by side.

They're covered in a blanket of red, orange, and yellow leaves, just like the rest of the forest. The only aspect that's recognizable as a gravesite are the duel rounded headstones sticking up. They're both a beautiful obsidian black, an exact match to a dire descendent's eyes. Engraved into them are two names, one for each stone.

Raines Sydney and Searna Dela

Carved into the stone below each of the names is a symbol I've seen before, and one that if I move my eyes a few inches to the left I can see in the living, breathing flesh. The same stigma that's branded into the back of Riot's neck: the snarling head of a dire wolf encased within a bold pentagon.

A mere three feet in front of me and six feet down lie Riot Sydney's parents.

Not only is he a dire descendent, but one with double the dose from both his mother and his father. Meaning he's more closely related to the original and now extinct species than I had thought.

The venomous words he said to Senya at the Citadel flash in my mind. "They killed our parents! Maybe if you weren't so far up his ass you'd see that."

This clue was obvious enough to give the strong hunch that his parents were dead. Hell, that's basically what he said himself. But something about looking at him sitting here, so dejected and crumbled, makes the grief feel fresh.

"Your parents," I pause abruptly. This is thin ice that shouldn't be treaded, but the curiosity is burning overtop of it like an oil fire. "How long's it been?"

His answer is quiet, painfully so. "Four years."

"I'm sorry," I whisper, laying my hand gently on his shoulder, the one without the mark. He doesn't lean into my touch like he usually does when he needs to feel it, though he doesn't pull away either. This small lack of action is frightening. It's a prime example of just how easy it would be for us to go back to the beginning.

"I don't want your pity," he grumbles bitterly.

His hostile tone, not to mention the rejection of my sympathy, snaps something small within me.

"I wasn't giving you my pity, I was being a decent fucking person," is what I want to say. But the teeth clamping down on my tongue stops me.

He's hurting, and badly. I can almost feel the ache of loss in my own chest due to the phantom touch of the mate bond. It's unimaginable, the sorrow he must be feeling.

Instead of lashing out, I try in vain to comfort him.

"You avenged them." I move around to his side, stepping closer to him. "Romanov got what he deserved. Although I guess that still doesn't make it ri-"

"I didn't do it for them," he says abruptly, cutting me off.

I pause, furrowing my eyebrows. "What?"

"The Hierarchy killed my parents. Not Romanov." He talks in short sentences, as if each piece of vague information should be explaining it to me perfectly.

My forehead creases with even more confusion and frustration. He acts as if it would kill him to say a word more than the bare minimum.

I stumble over my words, not even knowing where to begin. "Wait, what? The Hierarchy? If Romanov didn't then why did-"

"He turned my sister against me."

"That's why you killed him?" I ask, not skeptically, but quizzically.

"No."

I suppress the urge to let out a loud, angry groan. My voice is a bit shaky in order to keep it level. "Then why?"

He turns and looks up at me. His eyes are on the edge of a dangerous, surging black.

"I know that he threatened you." Those dark irises find mine and the sense of vulnerability they evoke make me want to shrink backwards. It's like he can see straight through my skull and right into the very thoughts stored there.

But I don't let myself crumple under his gaze, no matter how badly I'm tempted. "Yeah. So?" I counter, sincerely hoping my air of nonchalance is believable.

He stands up and squares his shoulders with mine. A faint shadow is cast over me, his body standing in the way of the rising sun. It makes me feel small in comparison to him. I can't decide whether I hate that or cherish it.

"He threatened your life if you didn't make sure I obeyed. I could have gotten you killed, Adrienne!" He growls, raising his voice an octave. The edge he had been balanced on is unbalanced now. And it tipped in the direction of anger.

Shame settles on my shoulders like gravity is pushing it down. I did nothing wrong and yet I'm being scolded, which in turn results in watered down flurries of pointless guilt. My gaze drops to the ground to study a peculiarly orange leaf.

As if realizing that I'm not going to feed his flame, his voice softens. "Why didn't you stop me? You knew what would happen if I stepped out of line."

I meet his eyes again, and for once sarcasm or a snide comment isn't the first thing I want to say. It's something sincere this time.

"I'm not going to control another person's life," I state firmly, "I know what that feels like and it fucking sucks."

As I continue, passion and pent up hatred from the past seeps out. "You should know what that's like. You said that the entire city acted like babysitters toward you. Well I had babysitters, too. One was a fickle Alpha and the other was a hardass guard that didn't speak a single word to me and whose backside I can still remember to this day. So no, I'm not, nor will I ever, tell you what decision to make."

I pause to take a breath, "Besides that I'm not your babysitter. Find somebody else for that job."

He stares back at me unfalteringly. There's not a single trace of a tear or any redness around his eyes. His pain is completely internalized. Just like every other emotion.

"Let's go," is all he says before walking away. My teeth grind together in agitation. Maybe I missed the point here. Or maybe he's just being a vague asshole to get on my nerves. If I had to bet money, I'd go with the latter.

I trail after him past the graves and further into the woods.

We hike uphill through the forest. Every step is more exhausting than the last. Although the cabin stands on a flat portion in a massive hillside, the main section of the mountain climbs higher.

Despite spending my life exploring the mountainous and heavily forested terrain of the Visari territory, my legs start to burn with fatigue. It's like the ground goes straight up in some places. At one point, Riot and I are both on our hands and toes, grabbing for roots and rocks buried in the dirt in order to heave ourselves up.

Finally, we reach the top. Riot rounds a massive ancient oak tree, one so huge I doubt if my arms could even reach halfway around. On the other side of the monstrous tree is a small flat area. Bushes and weeds stand high above my head, fully capable of swallowing me whole. I keep my eyes glued on Riot's back like he's a life raft floating through a storm at sea.

He stops and my head slams into his shoulder blade.

"What are you doing?" I ask, blinking to reclaim my sight.

"Look." He gestures in front of us and pulls aside a giant leafy weed. I'm guided forward by his hand on the small of my back. As soon as I can process what it is, my mouth drops open at the sight before me.

34 | Homesick

I t's like we're on top of the world, looking out across it. There's a vast sea of trees below— an entire valley of woods nestled in the basin of a circle of forest covered mountains. It's as if those mountains were hiding this place from the rest of the world, an impressive feat considering it's a world all its own.

"It's beautiful," I finally manage, at a complete loss for words. Beautiful doesn't even begin to describe it. There's something here, something in the air itself, that's eerily noticeable. There's a weird feeling swirling inside me just as indescribable as the place itself. Like power is radiating from the ground. Like something tragic took place here, lost within the grand scheme of time.

I'm astonished beyond utterance, but I'm still confused. "Why are you showing me this?"

He gives a small shrug. "You seemed homesick. I thought this kind of looked like your old territory." He's right. It does remind me a bit of the forests and mountainsides of Visari. Visari is a home that I can't go back to, a land I love with every ounce of my being. But not even Visari can compare to this.

The fact that Riot was thinking of me, of me missing my home, warms my heart. There's a little flutter in my chest, making me realize just how happy I am to be stuck with him. I may miss the place I grew up, but I would trade it for this any day. For a cabin hidden away in an unclaimed forest with my mate.

I smile and move toward him, wrapping my arms around his torso. "Thank you," I breathe into his collar bone. He hesitates a little before returning my hug. As if he didn't expect me to appreciate the gesture.

Over his shoulder, my eyes land on a massive strip of natural debris. It's an enormous landslide of boulders and dirt. Judging by the grass, weeds, and wildflowers that grow on it, it fell a long time ago.

An irrational and impulsive thought pops into my head. An image of me trapped beneath the landslide when it fell. Sealed off from any air besides the meager supply that was trapped with me. Air that I would waste by screaming and clawing at the rocks, trying to find a way out. All while ignoring the knowledge that if someone did hear me, they wouldn't be able to dig far enough to save me.

I find myself squeezing Riot tighter. Within his chest, his heartbeat speeds up, pounding in my ear. I look up at him with a gleam in my eye.

"You know I hate you, too, right?"

He chuckles a bit, pushing my hair back over my head. "I know."

I realize with a pang of excitement that he's smiling. A full blown, undeniable smile.

Holy shit I've witnessed history.

I've caught him grinning before, or even suppressing a smile. But never have I seen one as immensely happy as the one on presently on his face. And it's all because I hate him.

• • •

The trip back down the brutal mountainside is spent with me trying to use any method possible to accidentally make Riot fall the rest of the way down. So far, none of my attempts have succeeded.

He tries to counter my shenanigans with little pushes and shoves of his own, but his wolf scolds him before anything can happen.

About five minutes after I tried tossing a rock under his foot to trip him, his hand presses between my shoulder blades and gives me a swift little nudge. I lurch forward from the force, only to be immediately jerked back into place by his iron grip around my arm.

"Riot!" I shout through laughter, having been over this before. "It doesn't count if you catch me. We've been through this."

"This is a stupid game," he grumbles. He's clearly only grouchy because he's losing.

"Yeah? Well you have a stupid face."

I can feel him roll his eyes at the back of my head.

By the time the house comes into sight, the sun is fully up and it's got to be at least noon.

I'm studying the cabin from afar when I stop dead in my tracks. Riot bumps into me from behind. "What?" He asks, laying a hand on my shoulder to get my attention.

"Um..." I point awkwardly in the direction of the cabin. Someone is walking along the backside of it. Riot's eyes follow my finger just in time to see the figure slipping around the corner and out of sight.

His growl rumbles in his chest, and as a result sends vibrations traveling through my back. He then storms passed me and straight towards the house on a clearly marked war path.

"Shit," I curse under my breath, hurrying to catch back up.

I follow on his heels as he rounds the corner of the cabin, right where we'd seen the stranger go. When the front porch comes into sight, a boy is standing there. At the sound of dead leaves being stomped under our feet, he turns to face us.

"Who the hell are you?" I ask, trying to give him a chance to explain himself. Since my irrational comrade isn't much for talking, it's up to me to get as much information out of him as I can before Riot gets his hands on him.

Or not.

The stranger is slammed against the front door, held there by Riot's fist clenched around his collar. Fear flashes across the boy's tanned face and the bit of dirty blond hair across his eyes does nothing to hide it.

"I'm a-"

"Rogue," Riot finishes with a low growl. He loosens his hold on the rogue, as if somehow that vouched for his innocence. He nods at Riot in confirmation, silently thanking him.

I join them on the porch, coming up beside the both of them in order to inspect the rogue closer. To attempt to read his intentions through his eyes.

"Why are you here?" Riot snarls, stepping back to give him room against the front door he was previously pinned against.

"I heard what you done to Romanov. Everyone has." The boy seems to get a bit more comfortable now that canines aren't snapping in his face.

Riot looks at him skeptically, as if asking, "so what?" He truly doesn't realized how revered he is, be it through fear or admiration. And if he does, he doesn't care.

"You're the only wolf that's ever beaten him. You killed him," he speaks with awe in his voice. Almost like he idolizes Riot. Like a little kid with a gleam in his eye while meeting his childhood hero.

I audibly snort, earning a sideways glare from Riot as I try in vain to hold in my laughter. This has to be some kind of joke. Riot? An idol? Never.

Despite my skepticism, he seems serious. The longer he goes on, the more passionate he becomes. "That asshole has been hunting and cutting down rogues for years. He got what he deserved,"

"What's your point?" I interrupt before he can praise Riot further. If he's not careful it'll go to his head, then I'll be the one listening to his ego.

"I'm sick of having my self worth measured by how well I grovel at some Alpha's feet," he says, "And if I have to be in a pack then I don't want some mightier-than-thou prick at the top. You're a rogue. You should understand."

Like me, Riot snorts, almost laughing at those words.

"Did you miss the 'exiled' part of 'the Exiled Alpha?' Entering Balaige territory means death. No other pack smiles at me, either." There's a bitter lining to his tone. Bitterness towards having to admit the power he lost.

"No. I never said take over another pack. The packs have nothing to do with this. You don't need on their territory to run your own," the rogue replies slickly. He's thought this through, and thoroughly so.

Riot's eyes are cold as they gaze down on the boy standing on our doorstep seeking out his leadership. He can't be any more than fourteen years old, the very age Riot was when his parents took him to Khopeski. They have undoubtedly faced the same prejudices that come with being a rogue. The only difference is that one embraces it and the other wants out.

"Find a different Alpha," Riot says, and with that he turns him away.

• • •

Ever since we watched that boy walk away, Riot has been quiet. More so than usual. For the past seven days his eyes have often been blurry. Lost in his own thoughts while I try to guess them.

He's sitting on the leather couch, the very same one that's been put through the wall and flipped across the living room countless times. The fireplace burns brightly in front of him, giving light to the entire room. I roll over the back of the couch, plopping down in the seat next to him.

"I finally fixed the claw marks in the hall upstairs," I say, trying to sound happy over the tedious task with the hope that maybe it would wear off on him.

"Good," is all I get as he continues staring meaninglessly at the fire.

And that's when the last straw is pulled.

"Alright," I sit up straighter, "What's wrong with you? You've been brain-dead for a week, what's the deal?" I pin him with a weighted stare. He's not getting out of dodging this question. I've left him alone to sulk for long enough.

For the first time since that rogue disappeared back into the woods, Riot's eyes truly look at me. They aren't zoned out as they do nor are they clouded with underlying thoughts or disingenuous attention.

He's looking at me like the tyrant I've come to tolerate always has.

"Do you want your pack back, baby?"

Epilogue

Author's Note: Since I don't want anyone to hate me, I'm giving you guys a choice here...

If you want the happier ending, then stick with stopping at chapter 34. If you want to see the true ending, then continue reading the epilogue :)

Snow falls down from the grey sky. The sun is absent, smothered by heavy, electrified clouds. Each white flake dissolves upon hitting the ground, soaking into the rain puddles that had come hours before.

In the mud that was created, rogues still fight Visarian wolves— the few of them that are left. Amidst a clearing in the street of the tribal village, a girl is on her knees. Her clothes are sodden with rain, sweat, and blood. Her hair is just the same. Various shades of blonde strands hang limply around her face and shoulders.

She holds her hands up, palms facing the stormy sky as she stares at them. Not at them, but rather what's on them. Her hands are wet, stained with the crimson essence that came from the body laying in front of her. The body is a boy's, only one year older than the girl.

They were raised together. They were trained like Alphas together. They shared the same father until that father had to choose one of them, and he chose the one he had made.

Now that one lies dead, his blood on the other's hands.

Gage. That was the name written in marker on the palm of an abandoned baby. Now here she is, a baby no longer.

"Adrienne!" The girl's head snaps up at the sound of her name. Another girl is running towards her, tight brown curls bouncing on her head as she does.

"Aimee..."

Aimee drops to the ground beside Adrienne, crushing her in a forced hug. It's been well over a year since she last saw her best friend. Last winter, when the tyrant paid visit to their pack.

Now it's winter again, and so much has changed.

"I told them not to hurt you," Adrienne breathes into her friend's shoulder. Aimee only hugs her tighter.

"They didn't. I may have broke one's nose, but it's all good," she smiles, trying to lighten the grave situation. Her smile quickly falls when she acknowledges the body.

"So the narcissist is finally dead. What were his last words?"

"My father won't forget this. He'll do worse than lock you up," Adrienne recites, recalling the words from only moments ago.

Aimee snorts. "Even in the face of death he expected his daddy to solve his problems. Speaking of which, Alpha Andre... he ran."

Adrienne's slumping shoulders are suddenly pulled up straight. "He ran? That fucking cowardly bastard ran?" Her fists ball in her lap, claws extending. She chuckles bitterly, lividly, "I hope the wild rips him apart."

She senses a presence approaching. When she turns to find it, her eyes land on the very tyrant that made this all possible. He taught her what freedom is. Freedom beyond the gratefulness for the downtime between punishments.

Aimee grins in the satisfied way she always used to when she was proven right and Adrienne wrong. "What was it I said?" She feigns ignorance, flaunting her victory for all it's worth, "That Adrienne Gage would find somebody attractive one day?"

"Who says I find him attractive?" Adrienne asks, failing to hide her smile.

"Yeah okay," Aimee says as she stands back up, "I'll leave you two alone then. Come find me later." With an ornery smirk plastered on her face, she turns on her heel and goes.

Adrienne gets to her feet to meet her mate. Relief floods her chest like a broken dam. He's okay. He may be blood splattered with the face of a walking massacre, but he's been worse. Having singlehandedly conquered an entire pack twice before, he's more than experienced by the third occasion. He takes her head in both hands, pressing a kiss to her forehead once he reaches her.

"It's yours now," he tells her, looking into her eyes with an unreadable deepness in his own. The same deepness that hides all the thoughts she can never decipher.

Her brow furrows, confusion growing on her countenance. "What do you mean 'mine?' I'm not the tyrant here."

He shakes his head. "This is your pack, Adrienne. Your shit excuse of a father figure may not have meant for you to be the Alpha of it, but whatever ancestors or gods it is you look up to do."

Her face falls blank, mouth falling slightly open. Those aren't the words of a wolf who has just secured himself a new pack, nor the tone of an exile gaining back power once lost. No. It's the tone of someone who doesn't want to say what they have to next.

"Spit it out," Adrienne demands, driven mad by his silence. Anticipation isn't something she values, especially when caused by the person in front of her. His hands find their way to her waist before he obeys her order.

"I'm leaving."

She blinks at him. That simple phrase registering into her brain is like water mixing with oil: it doesn't. They have went everywhere together, from the day he took her away from the people who caused her so much abuse to the day they gave those people what they deserved. Leaving doesn't exist between them. The world turned on them both, so they become one.

"It's for your protection," he explains when her gaping mouth fails to form words, "You know what happened in Khopeski. People hunt tyrants. I'm not putting their attention on you. This place is small enough and hidden enough to keep quiet. If I'm not here, it should stay that way."

Adrienne scoffs, shaking her head in disbelief. Ever since he conquered Visari for the first time, she's been trying to analyze him. To sit in a front row seat and figure out the mystery behind him which the rest of the werewolf world never could. Now she's come to her final conclusion. "Riot, you're fucking insane."

Half of a smile cracks his lips. "Maybe. But you'll be safe. A Visarian rules Visari."

She wants to argue with him. She wants to call him names, to tell him that he doesn't have to leave. But she knows he's right. The world doesn't pay attention to Visari, and wherever the Exiled Alpha goes, a spotlight follows.

The distance between them evaporates as Adrienne pulls him into a crushing embrace. Her arms lock around his midsection and her face presses hard against his chest. She holds onto him tightly, like she never wants to let go. Because as soon as she does, he'll be gone.

"Stay. Please." She's never begged for anything before. She's held her ground and taken whatever punishment is to come. But this is worse than any punishment she's received. This is an exception.

Riot's copper eyes soften. He hugs her tighter, pressing a tender kiss to her lips. Even without words, Adrienne has learned to read what he's saying.

"Promise me you'll be back." Her voice is muffled against his body, but he hears her plea perfectly.

"I promise. I'll be back," he says, and he's never meant anything more. He knows the separation won't be long, but changes are always excruciating. It's painful; when the second half you've towed everywhere with you can no longer come.

"How long?" She asks.

"A month."

"Where?"

His answer this time makes her heart ache with longing. "The cabin."

It's the exact same cabin that acted as their refuge. The one where they had bonded. The one whose interior had withstood the wrath of his torment until she had taught him it's okay to feel something besides hatred. Now he would be going back alone and she would be staying here, attempting to become the Alpha her younger self was trained to be.

It takes an extraordinary strength to separate, and when they finally do they do so with mutual reluctance. With one last look at her grey eyes and one last parting squeeze of her hand, he turns and he goes, leaving her to cherish the memory of how it feels to be pressed against his body.

A knot forms in her throat, a wave of grief repressed in the heart of her chest as she watches him go.

"I hate you, Riot Sydney." Her quiet voice breaks as hot liquid warms her eyes.

He hears her, making the task all the harder. He looks back over his shoulder, a sad smile on his face.

"I hate you, too," he says. Nothing could ever be more opposite than the statement they exchange with each other.

Riot Sydney has a great power. He has the ability to affect people's lives. Every path he crosses, he alters. Like a streak of lightning disrupting the sky, or a tear ripping the fabric apart. Just like all destructive things, he doesn't notice his affect. And if he does, he doesn't care.

He caused problems in Khopeski both times he was there. He overtook Balaige within a day and cut them off from the outside world for three years. He evoked fear in every pack wolf with just the whisper of his name as an exile.

He slaughtered the only person who was relied upon to bring him down. And as for Visari, he wiped them out, though not before toying with their Alpha's dominance first.

He saved a certain Visarian from whatever deteriorating life she would have had under a narcissist's watch. He gave her a pack to lead, one taken from her before she was even born. He's touched every living and late werewolf's existence, either directly or otherwise.

And he doesn't notice any of it as he walks away from yet another life he's shaken. Except this time, he plans on walking back.

-